Dragonholder

Dragonholder

Todd J. McCaffrey

DEL REY

THE BALLANTINE PUBLISHING GROUP • NEW YORK

A Del Rey® Book
Published by The Ballantine Publishing Group

Copyright © 1999 by Todd J. McCaffrey
Foreword copyright © 1999 by Anne McCaffrey

www.randomhouse.com/delrey/

Library of Congress Cataloging-in-Publication Data
McCaffrey, Todd J.
Dragonholder / Todd J. McCaffrey.—1st ed.
p. cm.
"A Del Rey book"—T.p. verso.
ISBN 0-345-42217-1 (hc : alk. paper)
1. McCaffrey, Anne. 2. Women novelists, American—20th century
Biography. 3. Fantasy fiction—Authorship. 4. Science fiction—
Authorship. 5. Pern (Imaginary place) 6. Dragons in literature.
I. Title.
PS3563.A255Z77 1999
813'.54 99-31283
[B]—DC21

Text design by Debbie Glasserman

Manufactured in the United States of America

First Edition: November 1999
10 9 8 7 6 5 4 3 2 1

To Betty and Ian Ballantine,
whose kindness, faith, and perseverance did
more than give us the dragons
of Pern—they kept them flying.

Author's Acknowledgments

This book would not have been written but for Shelly Shapiro of Random House/Del Rey. It was at her suggestion that I started it at all.

I would like to thank Betty Ballantine, David Gerrold, and Virginia Kidd for consenting to be interviewed for this book. My thanks to Carolyn A. Davis, the Reader Services Librarian in the Department of Special Collections of Syracuse University, for providing me with a copy of Anne McCaffrey's original *Dragonflight* notes. I would also like to thank Don Maitz and Halley Erskine for kindly allowing me to include photographs they took.

I would also like to thank my sister, Georgeanne Kennedy, and brother, Alec Johnson, for their recollections and encouragement. Thanks also to my very good friend Geoff Hilton for allowing me to tell a very good tale on him, and to Derval Diamond for the same reason. And I'd like to thank all our friends in Ireland for their kindness and support.

I could not have written this without the support of my wife, Jenna, and the love of my daughter, Ceara.

Author's Acknowlegments

My debt to Anne McCaffrey, my mother, goes far beyond this book and no acknowledgment will ever be sufficient. In addition to all that has gone before, I would like to thank you, Mum, for putting up with my interviews and the countless E-mail exchanges for this book.

Needless to say, any mistakes, omissions, or downright lies are strictly my own.

Todd J. McCaffrey

17 March 1999

Cead mille Failte

Introduction

Cead mille Failte—a thousand welcomes, as they say here in Ireland. I've had the pleasure of greeting many of my readers at my house and while I'd love to greet each and every one of you, there'd be no time for writing—and you wouldn't want that!

So, for those that can't come here, and to free myself up for the serious task of writing, we decided to build you a scrapbook of tidbits and pictures. To let you get the feel of things, as it were. It's the same scrapbook we'll be showing my grandchildren as they get older.

I've asked my number-two son, Todd—the same Todd as in *Decision at Doona*—to do the work for me. It's nothing he hasn't done before. In fact, if anyone were to write about Pern, it'd be him.

So settle back, put your feet up, don't mind the cat, and turn the page!

Anne McCaffrey
Dragonhold-Underhill
April 1999

When I was nine years old, I started reading science fiction. My first book was *Space Cat* by Ruthven Todd. I really loved the whole Space Cat series. I loved it so much that I decided to write a fan letter to the author. He never replied. My mother was upset by that and vowed to answer all her fan mail.

She still does to this day. Her first fan was an eighty-year-old veteran of the Royal Flying Corps of World War One, named Pat Terry. He was paralyzed from the waist down and had to write lying on his back with a notepad held at arm's length. With such dedicated fans as him, it was not at all hard to find the time to respond. As the number of her fans increased, my mother had to spend less time responding to fan mail—or else spend less time writing the new books every letter clamored for!

I remember her proudly showing me her copy of *The Magazine of Fantasy & Science Fiction* with "The Lady in the Tower" in it. All I saw was a magazine with a picture of a banana floating on a field of stars— nothing at all like the picture of a cat romping in a spacesuit on the moon.

As the years passed (and her covers got better) I became a voracious reader of Anne McCaffrey. I even claim the distinction of being the very first person to read the individual pages of *The White Dragon* as it came out of Mum's IBM Selectric typewriter.

While you've been to Pern—met Lessa in her lonely fight against Fax, cried with joy for the smallest dragonboy, marveled at Robinton's wit and humor, laughed with Menolly and her gay ways—you haven't heard the stories behind the stories.

I propose to fix that.

I suppose we ought to get acquainted, oughtn't we? I am Todd Johnson McCaffrey, Anne McCaffrey's middle child. I am the person who, aged twelve, writhed with anticipated teenaged taunts when his mother suggested dedicating *Decision at Doona* "To my darling son, Todd." We settled on "To Todd Johnson—of course!"

All Anne's kids are "A" children, but while Alec and Gigi (Georgeanne) were born in August, I joined her in April. I arranged this by the rather unique expedient of being born more than a month late. For some reason, we kids were all inclined to the late twenties; Alec was born on the twenty-ninth and Gigi and I were both born on the twenty-seventh of our respective months. Sadly, this means that I missed my mother's famous April Fool's birth date.

Growing up, I was the first of Anne's children to read science fiction. Because of this, I went with her to many meetings with her fellow writers, editors, publishers, and agent, and also to several of the local science fiction conventions.

I remember once being refused entrance to our front room in Sea Cliff, Long Island, because Anne was brainstorming. And what did I think about dragons? she asked. Why dragons? I asked. Because they've had bad press all these years, was the answer. I went away very confused.

Writing is a strange job—both very lonely and very social. A whole new world inhabited with marvelous people in desperate situations is created, examined, and brought to life solely by oneself. A writer now myself, I am coming to understand those intense feelings of having people who are determined to be created knocking around inside your head.

In Sea Cliff, most of Anne's work was not done in the front room. She had a narrow room at the back of the first floor that was filled with books, filing cabinets, a table, a bed, and a typewriter—first a Hermes, later an IBM Selectric.

The house at 369 Carpenter Avenue, Sea Cliff, Long Island, was an old three-story Victorian. Old is a relative term; this house was about eighty years old when we moved in back in 1965. We shared its eighteen rooms and ten bathrooms with the Isbells, another Du Pont family—my father worked for Du Pont—who had also relocated from Wilmington, Delaware. It wasn't a commune, merely a practical way that two families could afford to live in that very expensive part of New York.

We split the house, with a front room for each family and shared access to the great dining room on special occasions like Christmas. It was a good, if sometimes difficult, arrangement. The Isbells had the

Gigi, Alec, and me (1960)

369 Carpenter Avenue

*Gladys "Aunt Gladdie" Norton
McElroy and John McElroy*

front entrance, the first-floor kitchen, and most of the second floor, while we had the side entrance, the whole of the third floor, some of the second, and Anne's room in the back of the first floor.

There Anne wrote all the stories that would be collected as the novel *Dragonflight* and wrote her first attempt at its sequel, which her agent told her to burn—and she did. It was from Sea Cliff that she first ventured to Ireland, in 1968, accompanying her favorite aunt, Gladdie.

Aunt Gladdie was a hoot. She was an outgoing, kind person and we all loved her very much. Anne only found out on their European trip that Gladdie had suffered all her life from a spinal condition that caused her a great deal of pain. Gladdie dulled the pain by liberal application of alcohol, normally in the form of Scotch on the rocks; but any whiskey could be used in a pinch.

Gladdie stayed with us one Christmas at Sea Cliff. I recall that on New Year's Day, all the adults in the house—except my mother—were very "fragile" in the morning. Apparently they'd stayed up all night with Aunt Gladdie, trying to match her drink for drink. They'd failed. Gladdie cheerfully arrived for breakfast and nearly got throttled when, taking in their condition, she said sympathetically, "You know, I don't think I'd drink so much if I ever got a hangover!"

When Anne was younger, Gladdie would invite her up to her home in Winthrop, Massachusetts, for holidays. She felt that Anne didn't get as much attention as she needed. This was because Anne's younger brother had been hospitalized with osteomyelitis—an often fatal disease in those days before penicillin—and Anne's mother acted as his private nurse. Among other treats, when Anne was sent to Stuart Hall, Aunt Gladdie sprang for the piano lessons Anne had begged for.

"She was the first person who had faith in me for myself alone," Anne says of her.

After I left the front room that day (a number of years before Aunt Gladdie took Anne to Ireland and at least a whole summer before Gladdie drank everyone under the table), and Anne had decided on dragons, she set about figuring out what sort of planet they were on. She'd had two stories published in John W. Campbell's magazine, *Analog*, and had had a number of meetings with him. Under John's vision, *Analog* (known as *Astounding Science Fiction* until 1960) had become the premier science fiction magazine of the 1950s and 1960s, specializing in character-driven hard science fiction stories. So Anne was concerned not only with the story but also with the science and the background.

She settled on a technologically regressed survival planet, existing in near-medieval times. Because America was so divided over the Vietnam War at that time, Anne wanted a world unified against a common, undeniable enemy. So she came up with Thread: mindless, voracious, space-borne. The dragons became the biologically renewable air force, and their riders "the few" who, like the RAF pilots in World War Two, fought against incredible odds day in, day out—and won.

Anne finished thinking and returned to her back room and the typewriter. Hours later, after writing all of *Weyr Search* up to the fight scene, she took a break to finish the prom dress for Linda Isbell, the daughter of our housemates. At Sea Cliff the magical and the mundane were mixed; a scraped knee might interrupt Lessa's Impressing Ramoth. Somehow Anne found the time to cook, to sew—and to let dragons fly.

When she had done what she could with the story (long after the prom), Anne took the unfinished *Weyr Search* and two other stories with her up to the writers' conference at Milford, Pennsylvania. She gave *Weyr Search* and another story to her agent, Virginia Kidd, and submitted the third to the judgment of the writers' group. Harlan Ellison, now famous for so many things—*Star Trek*'s "City on the Edge of Forever," *The Outer Limits*'s "Demon with a Glass Hand," the *Dangerous Visions* anthologies, and the classic novella "A Boy and His Dog"—

Harlan Ellison (standing)

but then science fiction's reigning bad boy, tore Anne's submission apart. Anne was used to Harlan's ways and rewrote the story. It was later published as "A Womanly Talent"—the second story in *To Ride Pegasus*.

Virginia read the incomplete "Weyr Search" and handed it back, saying, "Oh, Annie, *do* please finish it." When Virginia submitted the completed story to John Campbell at *Analog*, he bought it. He wanted more.

Virginia? Anne will tell you that she first met Virginia in the local supermarket at Milford. At the time Virginia was Virginia Kidd Blish, married to the science fiction writer James Blish, who was best known then for his Cities in Flight series but may be better known now for his *Star Trek* novelizations.

Anne? Virginia will tell you that she was "given" Anne by Judy Merril. Judy Merril was so impressed with Anne's second-ever story, "The Lady in the Tower," that she invited Anne up to her first "Milford"—the local writers' conference. "The Lady in the Tower" had been published in *The Magazine of Fantasy & Science Fiction* (known to all as "*F&SF*"), edited at the time by Robert P. Mills. He published the story after associate editor Algys "AJ" Budrys—another writer/editor—had pulled it from the slush pile. Judy, who herself had been married to science fiction writer/editor Frederik Pohl, was at the time editing *The Year's Best Science Fiction* and discovered, amidst the many published stories under consideration for inclusion in the anthology, "The Lady in the Tower."

In science fiction and fantasy in the 1940s, 1950s, and even the late 1960s, everyone knew everyone else. There was and still is a strong sense of community in the profession and a willingness to help new writers starting out.

Most of the magazine editors in the old days started life as writers. Many did a stint of editing and returned to writing. While they were editing, they looked out for ways to help beginners, too, the way Sam Moskowitz helped Anne.

Anne's first story, "Freedom of the Race," was bought by Sam for *Science Fiction Plus*. He did Anne a big favor by cutting the story from 1,300 words to 1,000 words. Why was that a favor, you might ask? In those days *Science Fiction Plus* paid the glorious amount of three cents per word. The longer the story, the more the author got paid.

But at that time there was a story competition for the best 1,000-word story, and *that* paid $100. By cutting the story by three hundred words, Sam made Anne's story jump in value from $39 to $100.

Judy Merril had noticed Anne's second story, "The Lady in the Tower," and bought it for her *Year's Best* anthology. From her contact with Anne, Judy knew that she was looking for an agent; she also knew that Virginia had decided to start agenting, so she introduced them. They hit it off and they've been together ever since.

Just as important as Judy's introduction of Anne to Virginia was Judy's invitation to Anne to attend her first Milford writers' conference in 1959. It was called "Milford" because it was held in Milford, Pennsylvania. The Milfords were originated by Damon Knight, James Blish, and Judy Merrill—all three being science fiction writers, editors, and sometime critics. The idea was to gather the brightest writers in the field together for a number of weeklong, intense rounds of criticism. Every writer brought a story to the conference, all the writers read all the stories, and all participated in the critiquing of the stories. Anne says she learned more about the craft of writing at Milford—she returned to the conference many times—than anywhere else.

She couldn't stay long at her first Milford because she was pregnant with her third child, who would be named Nicholas if a boy, or Georgeanne if a girl—in those days the doctors couldn't tell.

She nearly didn't get there at all because her second child—me— almost scared her into early labor. This was back in Wilmington, Delaware, where we had a really great split-level bungalow house. One of the few problems it had was that the house was at a major intersection in the housing development. Another problem was that it fronted onto a hill. It wasn't much of a hill, unless you were a three-year-old, in which case it was a mountain.

The hill wouldn't have been a problem for me except that my mother, our Anne, had this vision of her children growing up and having children of their own (she succeeded). Fortunately for her, we had some really smart dogs—German shepherds. The first, Wizard, was the father of the second, Merlin.

Now, Wiz was so smart that after Anne walked him around the property line he knew what was his and where his child was allowed to go. And where his child wasn't—like down the hill and onto the busy main road. So every time I tried to go down, he'd get in front of me. I'd go around; he'd get in front. And because a three-year-old just can't walk around an eighty-pound dog, I'd always go back up the hill, toward the house, when I tried to get around. My brother thought it was hilarious, my mother thought it was great, but I thought it was too much.

Okay, I was only three and didn't know better. But even back then I

Anne McCaffrey, Gordon Dickson, Hal Clement,
and Ben Bova (1969)

100 Danforth Place, Wilmington, DE

Me, Gigi, Anne, and Merlin

had stubborn all worked out. I knew that I couldn't get down to the road unless I was in a car. Hmm . . .

So one day I climbed into the car, got behind the wheel, and "Vroom! Vroom!" 'd a bit until I noticed the parking brake. My mother realized that it was too quiet just a bit too late and rushed out of the house in time to see me in the car rolling backward down onto the main street. At the same time our neighbor across the street saw Anne, huge with child, and yelled, "Anne! Don't run!"

Sir Isaac Newton was once again proved correct as the car rolled down our hill, across the main road, into the neighbor's driveway, *through* their garage door, and into their garage. Where our kindly neighbor managed to grab the parking brake. A kid's got to try, right? And you wonder where Anne McCaffrey ever got the idea to write *Decision at Doona*?

But that was the only time I *ever* got around Wiz. He was a very smart dog. He was a big German shepherd and quite intimidating. Once a workman came to Anne and said, "Lady, you've got to do something about your dog."

The workman was running a bulldozer a few doors down, digging a ditch or something. Anne looked out her back window and saw that Wiz was sitting in front of the bulldozer. "He won't move," the workman said. Anne went outside and saw that I was playing in the backyard. Then she looked again, smiled, moved me back toward the house a few feet, and called out, "Wiz! It's okay."

Wizard took one look and gave up his "dogged" vigil. His charge had been moved out of direct line with the bulldozer, so the bulldozer was no longer a threat. Wizard's son Merlin would later be remembered in Anne's gothic, *The Mark of Merlin,* and Wizard was given place of honor in the short story "The Great Canine Chorus."

Neither of those stories had been written back in 1959, when Anne went to her first Milford. While art may not imitate life, life was a major influence in Anne's art. Her first story, about women impregnated by aliens, was written when she was pregnant with her first child. Her second story, "The Lady in the Tower," was written when she had two children under six and a sixteen-year-old refugee from the aftermath of the Hungarian revolution living with her. Anne explained that she thought of the story when wishing herself alone, like a lady in an ivory tower.

Her third story, "The Ship Who Sang," was written almost as an elegy for her father.

Built upon her Milford experience and poignant memories of her father, this story was Anne's first *special* story. It is still special to her today.

"Someone screamed when the dirt was shoveled back in. I'm told it was me, but I don't remember." That is how Anne describes her father's funeral. They played "Taps," the soldier's song of evening, and Anne could never hear it again without dissolving in tears. In the story, Helva sings that song as the last song the ship sang—her tribute to her fallen partner, and Anne's tribute to her fallen father.

It takes the sternest of wills or great acting to read "The Ship Who Sang" aloud from beginning to end without weeping. It was the first story of Anne's that has been credited with saving lives; many people coming to grips with lost limbs have found solace and the courage to persevere in the stories of Helva, the ship who sang.

Not everyone found "The Ship Who Sang" to his or her taste. When Anne's husband, Wright, caught her crying one night, he asked, "What's wrong?"

"I've just killed my hero," she replied through her tears.

"Well, you're the writer, you don't have to do that," he said.

"No, I *had* to," Anne replied. "That's the way the story goes."

Wright left, shaking his head. It was a portent of things to come.

After "The Ship Who Sang," Anne's writing career went on hold. First, the family went to Germany for six months, following Wright's job. They rented an apartment in Düsseldorf, while Wright worked with Du Pont's public relations department to launch Teflon as a new fabric. Anne decided wisely to put the two school-age boys into the local public school rather than try to locate a private English-speaking school. It worked out well: by summer the two blond-haired boys were wearing lederhosen and acting like natives.

Georgeanne was going on three at the time and stayed home with her mother. Fortunately, Anne met a woman at the supermarket, Gisela Quante, who was willing to baby-sit evenings and brush up on her English.

Somewhere in the six months, little "Gigi"—she got her nickname from an uncle who said of her, "Such a gorgeous George"—learned enough German that, one day, when separated from her mother at the local supermarket she could tell the clerks, "*Ich habe meine Mutti gefor-loren* [I've lost my mother]."

Ich habe meine Mutti geforloren

Gisela allowed Anne and Wright time to attend the very inexpensive German opera available. They had a marvelous time. Anne met a Canadian opera singer—a tenor—who took her on as a voice student.

Voice? Well, now we'll have to go back more in time. In fact, to understand Anne, you have to know something of her ancestors.

A quick tour:

Anne's father, George Herbert McCaffrey, was the only son of George Hugh McCaffrey. George Hugh was a Boston cop at a time when the Irish were just getting out of the ghettos and the Jews were just entering. But George had integrity—he once arrested John F. Kennedy's grandfather, "Honey" Fitzgerald, for electioneering—and the Jewish merchants on his beat appreciated the way that he would

G. H. McCaffrey on his high school graduation

Anne Dorothy McCaffrey, nee McElroy

Mrs. McElroy felt her daughter had married beneath her.

allow no shenanigans. They were so impressed that they took up a collection to send his son, George Herbert, known as "GH," to Roxbury Latin School. George Herbert excelled and got a scholarship to Harvard. He graduated magna cum laude [with great praise]. He was granted a scholarship for postgraduate work, and the merchants added enough to it that he could work toward a doctorate in government—until World War One intervened.

GH entered the war as a lieutenant and fought in the infantry of the Seventy-eighth "Lightning" Division in France. After the war, he went to Poland to help set up their government. On his return to Boston, he met Anne Dorothy McElroy.

Anne Dorothy McElroy was the daughter of a New York printer/engraver who had emigrated to the States from Ireland via Scotland. While in those days there was only enough money to send her elder brother, John—who later married our favorite aunt, Gladdie—to college, Anne was educated well enough to be fluent in French and was more than able to add languages at will.

While Mrs. McElroy felt that her daughter would be marrying beneath her—after all, GH was the son of a policeman—Mr. McElroy did not share her views. And so, Anne Dorothy McElroy became Mrs. McCaffrey.

GH kept a reserve commission in the Army, attending drills monthly and drilling his own kids on the weekend. He was employed by the Commerce and Industry Association of New York, working on city and business planning. His doctorate, received in 1938, was "The Integration and Disintegration of Metropolitan Boston" and is, we're told, still being referenced in courses on government taught at Harvard.

Before the Depression, his job moved him down to New York City, so the family bought a house in Montclair, New Jersey.

Our Anne was the middle child of GH and Anne, between an elder brother, Hugh ("Mac"), and a little brother, Kevin ("Kevie"—shortened to "Keve" when he got older). As children and long after, Mac and Anne detested the sight of each other. Fortunately, I'm happy to say, they reconciled one night when Anne was about thirty-five.

It's hard to say why they disliked each other so much, and Mac was certainly very contrite about the whole thing whenever I mentioned it to him, but it might have had something to do with Anne's description of herself: "I was a brat."

Anne says that she grew up with no friends and was rebellious at school, and that her mother despaired of her ever finding a place in this world. Anne remembers that, as a youngster, because she had few friends, she took to dressing up the cat. Now, this particular cat was Thomas-cat who was a Maine coon that the family had rescued. If you've read *Decision at Doona* you will probably realize that the tail-pulling Todd has more than a passing relationship to the cat-dressing Anne. And I think that the Hrrubans owe their existence in no small part to Thomas-cat.

Thomas was special. When the family first found him, he was in sad shape and wouldn't eat. Anne's mother tried tempting the cat with everything, finally going to the extent of a rare cut of beef. When the cat still wouldn't eat, Anne's Grandmother McElroy scolded it, "You go right back over there and eat every bit." And to everyone's surprise but hers, Thomas did just that.

Thomas would put up with young Anne's dressing him in doll clothes and wheeling him around in a stroller until he would finally get fed up, jump out, and shed all the clothes on the ground.

Thomas was also friends with the next-door neighbor dog, a Terhune collie. When they first met, Thomas showed Rookie his house and kitchen, and the dog showed Thomas *his* house and kitchen—and they were inseparable. Thomas went so far as to convince Rookie to escort gruff old Grandmother McElroy when she went out for her walks, because she was terrified of dogs. The collie would follow discreetly behind her, keeping any of the neighbor dogs away.

When the dog caught a chill and died, Thomas *knew* before the vet called Rookie's owner. He rushed over to their house and was already comforting Rookie's mistress when the phone rang.

Anne D. McCaffrey,
Kevin, Hugh, and
Anne (seated)

At the end of his life, Thomas had a stroke. He went blind and his back legs were paralyzed. He tried to cope for a while, but finally it was too much. One day he pulled himself in front of Mrs. McCaffrey and rolled over, feet in the air, making it plain that he could endure no more.

Thomas had a lasting impact on Anne; we grew up with cats, as well as dogs, all around us. Recently, Anne acquired a breeding Maine coon cat in Ireland, and now Dragonhold-Underhill is the home of many.

As with our dogs, our cats moved in and out of our lives. In our Windybush neighborhood in Wilmington, Delaware, we had Touché, Tallabar—named in part after the previous cat, Cinnabar—and Silkie Blackington. Touché was a marvelous tortoiseshell male who died very young; Tallabar was a multicolored tortoiseshell who later sired a beautiful orange marmalade male, Maxwell Smart (named for his great lack of intellectual prowess).

Silkie was almost all black; she had the softest fur and the sweetest disposition. She sired three or four litters before we finally had her spayed. She got immensely fat but lived to the great age of fourteen. While she was officially Gigi's cat, when we moved up to Sea Cliff she split her nights equally between Gigi's bed on the third floor and Anne's in the back room on the first floor. Silkie had most of her litters in Anne's first-floor room.

Anne, Hugh, and Kevin

Anne with Zeus and Zorro

Todd with Touché in Wilmington, DE

*D*id I say a quick tour? There's more . . .

Anne was introduced to books as a young child. Her parents read to her every night. Rudyard Kipling was a featured author; her father would read the kids *The Jungle Book* and *Kim* and declaim *Barrack-Room Ballads* from down the hall when they were sick and had to be sheltered from bright lights. GH did not neglect Kipling's poetry, and Anne had no problem reciting "Gunga Din" from memory by the time she was in high school.

The Depression was not the major trauma to the McCaffreys that it was to so many others in that era. Mrs. McCaffrey had "had a feeling" about the stock market a few days before the crash and had pulled all her money out. For the next few days GH had chided her foolishness—but he got very quiet when the market crashed.

"Feelings" or "the Sight" are common to the McElroys–McCaffreys. Anne's grandfather McCaffrey (the policeman), a man of robust good health, unexpectedly called the priest for last rites three days before his death. Anne's Grandmother McElroy, the one who scolded Thomas-cat when he wouldn't eat, had a more alarming encounter.

When her sister, Anne, passed away, Grandmother McElroy became obsessed with worry about how her sister would find the afterlife—this particular Anne having never been very happy in life. The best Grandaunt Anne ever said of anything was, "Oh, it's not bad."

Grandmother McElroy prayed so hard to know if Grandaunt Anne was all right that her sister's ghost appeared before her at the front of her bed, shawl tucked into her clasped hands. Shocked to silence by the manifestation, it was some time before Grandmother finally managed to ask the relevant question.

"Oh, it's not bad," was the shade's diffident reply. At which point, Grandmother McElroy was so overcome by her success that she banished the vision and never dared use her abilities again.

Anne and her mother were a team on "knowing" things. The first time Anne ever had the Sight was in the summer of 1938 when Hugh was in summer camp and GH was on maneuvers at Fort Dix. When the phone rang, Mrs. McCaffrey exclaimed, "Something's happened to GH."

*Anne with brothers
Kevin and Hugh,
and mother Anne.
January 1942*

"No, it's Hugh," Anne replied. It was. He'd been rushed to the hospital with a dangerously inflamed appendix.

Between the Depression and World War Two, a major family tragedy befell the McCaffreys. Anne's younger brother, Kevin, came down with an undiagnosed illness. He began a long series of hospitalizations as doctors tried to diagnose the ailment. When they finally did, the news was the worst: it was osteomyelitis, an incurable infection of the bone marrow.

No one knew if Kevin was going to live or die. GH turned down an active duty commission as a colonel in the infantry as the US Army grew in preparation for war. Mrs. McCaffrey stayed with Kevin at the hospital, and Anne was sent to Stuart Hall school for girls. It had been established in 1844 as the Virginia Female Institute but was renamed in 1907 in honor of Headmistress Flora Cooke Stuart—J. E. B. Stuart's widow. Stuart Hall was an excellent choice for the daughter of a military man.

But before she was sent off to school, Anne experienced something that would stick in her memory forever and influence all her future writing. She recalls,

"When Keve was first ill and undiagnosed, he was given a variety of the sulfa drugs, which were all that was available to treat an unknown infection. What was eventually discovered, in the first of many operations on Keve, was that the infection started just below the kneecap in the tibia of the left leg.

"Mother was a constant companion and nurse for him, but the months when she didn't know what Keve had had drained her of energy. One night she asked me to sit up with Keve so that she could have a full night's sleep. I was to wake her if Keve was too restless; the drugs sometimes had that effect.

"I couldn't have been more than thirteen, for it was May. I was rather 'puffed up' to think that I could be allowed to help.

"It was a weird night . . . with Keve climbing endless mountains in his sleep with his hands, and throwing his head from side to side. His swollen leg was secured so that he couldn't injure it.

"Then, fighting sleep, I remember praying to keep awake. I was grateful when the early morning light seeped through the curtains. The curtains stirred—and suddenly I felt a 'something'—and Keve stopped his restless movements and fell deeply asleep. So deeply, at first, that I thought he had stopped breathing, although I *knew* that he was all right. The 'something' had reassured me about that.

"Later that day when the doctor came, he said that the crisis he had been waiting for had passed and Keve would be all right now. But I knew already, the 'something' had told me."

They did not know at the time that this would be the first of many crises.

The "something" Anne felt that night pervades her writing, never quite visible but always present. And always her style lets us know that no matter what the dangers, "something" will be watching over the characters in Anne's books, and they'll always make it through to the end.

Kevin was very brave throughout his ordeal. Once, when he was being moved to a different hospital, the ambulance men hustled him back inside because a hearse was driving by. Kevin—who couldn't have been more than twelve—told them, "Never mind, I'll be there soon enough."

Years later, Anne was to honor his bravery in "The Smallest Dragonboy"—a story that has become her most reprinted short work.

Anne's stint at Stuart Hall was set in motion on 7 December 1941, when the Japanese attacked Pearl Harbor. She had been out riding—her mother had gifted her with the use of a horse for the whole month—and passing motorists had shouted out the news of the attack. She rushed home to find her father and mother listening grim-faced to the radio reports of the attack. GH immediately phoned Army headquarters in New York and told them that he would serve in any capacity for which they felt him qualified.

The Army accepted and in January he was posted to Moultrie Advanced Air Force Base in Georgia as the base's quartermaster at his reserve rank of lieutenant colonel. Before he left, he paid a visit to Kevin at the hospital. At the time Kevin was in a full body cast in an attempt to treat the illness through immobilization. When her father left the hospital, Anne was shocked to see him in tears.

Gruff, stern, and insistent were the qualities most remembered by his children. GH, or the "Kernel," as he was now signing his letters, was a disciplinarian of the old school. He was a precise, neat man who hated confusion and disorder. He had a dry sense of humor. He tended to be choleric, but usually with cause. He had a graduated series of expletives—"Damn it," "Goddammit," and "Goddamitall to hellingone"—the severity of which indicated when the children should make themselves scarce.

The Kernel was *never* seen crying. Except now, leaving a son he might never see alive again.

Stuart Hall and Anne McCaffrey were not a good fit. A Northerner in a Southern school was a problem in itself; a *headstrong* Northerner who was also a Catholic was a sure recipe for trouble with the dean of women. While Anne was allowed to attend Mass, she was also required to attend the Episcopalian services in school. She learned more from the padre than she ever had from a priest or a nun and that, coupled with her crisis of faith in a God who would allow small children the horror of total war and incurable disease, started her break with Catholicism.

Stuart Hall was completely shocked when Anne insisted that she wanted to see the movie *Tarzan* in the nearby town. No chaperone could be found, and her wish marked her even more as a "rebel." (She did see the movie, and was disappointed; in her estimation, it did not live up to the books.)

However, Anne was an honors pupil, allowed to wear the school seal, and performed in the choir and the theater, taking the role of the Major General in *The Pirates of Penzance*. And, of course, she had her aunt Gladdie's gift of a year of piano lessons.

Anne had written her first story, "Flame, Chief of Herd and

Track," when she was nine and her second, "Eleutheria the Dancing Slavegirl," in Latin class. At Stuart Hall she wrote poetry. Lots of it. She spent hours pondering the perfect pen name and sent several poems in to the magazines, but none were ever published.

It was at Stuart Hall that Anne had an experience that haunted her then, and profoundly shaped her future. The Kernel had been sent from Moultrie AFB to the Military Governor's course at the University of Virginia. In May 1943, he disappeared, shipped overseas.

Lessa woke, cold.

Anne recalls,

"I woke abruptly—at about 3:00 A.M.—and terribly worried. Sick worried. I was so sick with worry that I wandered the halls, trying to keep from being seen by the night watchman because I shouldn't have been out of my little room. There was no way I could reach my mother, and I just didn't know what was wrong—but something very much was.

"At about 4:30, I was overcome with sleep and just made it back to my room.

"The next morning the dean sent for me. There was a call from my mother. The whole school knew that the Kernel had been sent overseas.

" 'Anne, did anything happen to you last night?' my mother asked. 'Kevin's all right but something is very, very wrong. I'm told that Hugh is well.'

"I said, 'It's probably Dad, then. I woke up at 3:00 and couldn't get back to sleep.'

" 'That's when I woke up,' Mother told me.

" 'Then at about 4:30 I fell asleep again.'

" 'Then it has to be your father . . .' Her voice trailed off. There was no way she could find out where the Kernel was.

"I tried to cheer her up. 'Well, the feeling went away, didn't it? So whatever it was is over.'

" 'Yes, yes, that's it. He's all right now,' Mother agreed, and hung up.

"Six months later we found out that German U-boats had attacked the convoy that took the Kernel to Algiers. He and the other top brass had spent an hour and a half in lifeboats—at exactly the same time that my mother and I had been so worried."

Cold with more than the chill of the everlastingly clammy walls. Cold with the prescience of a danger . . .

The Kernel survived his lifeboat experience, ordered a medical officer not to report his heart attack in Algiers, and was the first man off his landing craft in Licata, Sicily. The sight of him calmly walking up and down the jetty smoking a cigarette was an inspiration to the green GIs, and he was awarded a Beachhead medal. His first assignment was military governor of the town of Agrigento, Sicily.

In Agrigento the Kernel's Sight saved his life late one night as he was returning from a staff meeting. He and his driver were retracing the same route they had driven in daylight when the Kernel had a premonition. Peremptorily ordering the driver to stop, he got out of the

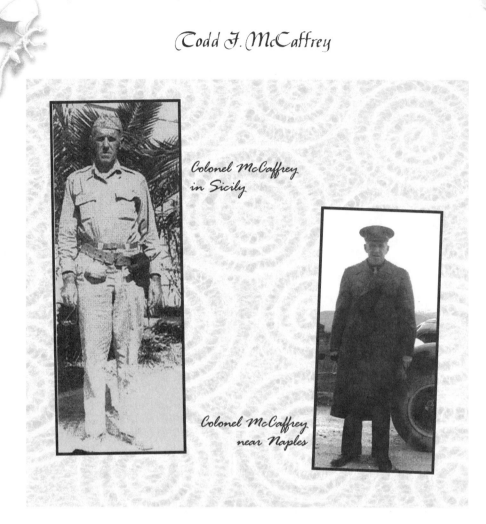

Colonel McCaffrey
in Sicily

Colonel McCaffrey
near Naples

jeep in the pitch darkness and, walking to the front, discovered that the bridge had been blown out. He later ordered the bridge rebuilt by Army engineers and it was known as Ponte del Caffreo.

Shortly after this incident a young reporter arrived to get some background color on the liberated Italians. He was directed to Agrigento and Colonel McCaffrey. He stayed on for a long while. During that time, General Patton started an advance out of Agrigento and was enraged to discover that the road into the town was used by the local water carts. Patton ordered that no more carts could use the road.

Agrigento sits up above the sea, with only one road running through it from the shore and continuing on inland. All the water for Agrigento came up that one road. Without the water carts, the thirty thousand inhabitants of Agrigento would have to abandon their town. Such an outcome would have disastrous repercussions both with the Sicilians and with the US public at home.

The Kernel made a hard decision. He countermanded General Patton's directive and ordered that the water carts continue their operations. When Patton heard about this he was furious. General Mark Clark agreed with the Kernel, and so the Kernel's counterorder remained in effect, but the colonel who countermanded a general's orders remained a colonel for the rest of his life.

To placate Patton, the Kernel was removed from Agrigento. In his place a Navy captain took over and continued in the same tradition. Ultimately the captain arranged to get a bell to replace the town's church bell, which had been shattered by the allied artillery. The reporter—John Hersey—stayed on and later wrote *A Bell for Adano*. His Colonel Joppolo is a blend of the Kernel and the captain.

While her father was leaving Agrigento, Anne was leaving Stuart Hall. The McCaffreys are not intimidated by authority and Anne was no exception. Stuart Hall would not let her graduate because she did not have two years of Bible study. So she finished high school back in New Jersey, being shunted from good neighbor to good neighbor, becoming as independent in bearing as she was in inclination.

The Kernel had gone to Harvard with Joseph Kennedy, both majoring in government. So it was natural enough that when Anne went to Harvard's sister college, Radcliffe, she met Robert Kennedy and went to parties at the Hyannisport compound.

Over some objections, "because the dean of women didn't think I was smart enough," Anne majored in Slavonic languages and literature.

She continued her stage work and performed at the college radio station, but found plenty of time for "real life"—that is, hanging out with friends at various restaurants around Harvard.

Hazen's was the most popular hangout for Anne; it was on the way from her dorm to her classes. And while Anne sat with her group of friends, Bobby Kennedy sat with his group of friends, mostly members of the college football team.

After the war ended, she was joined by her brothers for her last two years of college, during which time they were known as "Big Mac," "Mac," and "Little Mac."

s the war finished, the Kernel found himself working on the details of the military government of Austria. Once, he interrupted a high-level briefing commanded by General Mark Clark to report that the famous Lipizzaner mares that had been moved to Czechoslovakia at the start of the war were in danger of falling into

Soviet hands. Mark Clark, himself a rider, recognized their impor-
tance at once and authorized the Kernel to dispatch an armored col-
umn to snatch the mares out of Czechoslovakia just in front of the
advancing Soviets.

The Kernel had managed to pull rank on the medical officers from
Algiers, where he had his first coronary, and again in Sicily, London,
and Vienna, but he couldn't hide the diabetes that resulted from the
years of intense work, inadequate food, and stress. A severe attack suggested he'd better resign.

He returned to the States just before Anne's graduation. The war
had changed him so much that neither Anne nor Kevin recognized

*Colonel McCaffrey
is decorated by the
Czechs*

him. They rushed right by him while searching the crowd of return-ing soldiers.

The Kernel was a man of high standards. Occasionally he over-stepped himself. Anne's graduation ceremony was one rare occasion where he earned the wrath of his wife. Seeing that Anne had earned her degree cum laude [with praise] he *harrumphed* and said, "It should have been *magna*."

Anne's mother was incensed. "Who is this man?" she asked. "I don't know him."

*W*ell, there now—that was a bit more than a whirlwind tour, wasn't it? I hope now you know somewhat more of Anne as a child and young woman. Perhaps you've also a better insight into how she gets her ideas.

So, where were we? Voice. That's it.

Again on voice—as a little girl, when Anne wasn't going to be a writer, rider, or movie star, she was going to be a singer. As a child, she'd belt out songs when she was looking for attention. As she got older, her interests firmed.

At Stuart Hall she was the Major General in Gilbert and Sullivan's *The Pirates of Penzance*; at Radcliffe she perfomed in plays by Oscar Wilde, Sartre, and Chekhov. Anne didn't just sing and act; she tried to write an operetta based on the Irish tale *The Dream of Angus* and wrote a wacky song of which only this fragment remains:

"Chickory, chiggery chill

there's an awful lot of coffee in Brazil!"

Anne also added her voice to several radio plays on the local Radcliffe radio network.

After Anne graduated, she worked through a number of secretarial jobs in New York City until she secured a job at Liberty Music Shops as an advertising copy layout artist. Anne roomed with a radio actress and commercial writer, Betty Wragge of *Pepper Young's Family*, in an apartment catty-corner from Carnegie Hall and she dated a concert pianist. Customers at Liberty Music Shops included Rita Hayworth, Raymond Massey, Merle Oberon, and Tallulah Bankhead.

Tallulah was the most memorable. Anne was in the elevator with her and her boyfriend when the salesman mentioned that the new record players could play four and a half hours of music. Tallulah turned to her boyfriend with a twinkle in her eye and asked in sultry tones, "Dahling, do you think that will be long enough?"

In the summer, Anne did more theater work with the Lambertville Music Theatre, the first of the many tent theaters that became popular in the early 1950s. Anne worked with Wilbur "Wib" Evans, helping him to scale down operettas for smaller casts and choruses so that there would be a minimum number of people on the stage. But a stage wage was not as steady as her regular work, so Anne wrote off thoughts of a career on Broadway.

Wib and his wife, Susanna Foster, were two of the many people who were constantly introducing Anne to eligible bachelors. But it was still another older couple who introduced her to the handsome journalist who also had a penchant for music, opera, and ballet. He loved *The Beggar's Opera* and wooed her with it. When H. Wright Johnson proposed in September 1949, Anne accepted.

For most of the next nine years, Anne's singing and acting took backstage to her two children, her two science fiction stories, and her two moves. The first move was from their cold-water apartment in New York City to a rental house in Montclair, New Jersey—oddly enough, on "Normal Avenue." The second move brought the family to a new estate in Wilmington, Delaware, where right next door was a friendly family with a teenager old enough to baby-sit.

Anne joined the Breck's Mills Cronies and was the heroine's crony in their production of *The Vagabond King*. And she joined the Concord Presbyterian Church choir, singing soprano and taking lessons from the choirmaster, Ted Huang.

But the best was when Anne met the opera stage director of the Lancaster Opera Society. She first encountered him when they worked together on a production at the Wilmington Music School. They became fast friends, and he would often stop at her house for dinner after the long drive back to Delaware from Lancaster, Pennsylvania. Years later, Frederic H. Robinson, "Robie," would become the mold from which MasterHarper Robinton was cast.

The trip to Germany was a real wrench, as "Robie" had offered Anne a plum role in a modern opera. Worse, in Germany Anne's teacher, Canadian tenor Ron Stewart, decided that she was a contralto and commenced to train her in that lower range. It was a mistake. Singing in the lower range, Anne had flaws in the E, F, and G notes in the middle voice. Her maestro never allowed her to sing anywhere except in his studio, so she never noticed the flaw herself. When he finally told her about it, her devastation was traumatic.

Years later Anne bequeathed her emotions to Killashandra Ree, in *The Crystal Singer*: "I've repertoire! I've worked hard and now—*now* you tell me I've no voice!"

Back to Anne's parents. Bittersweet.

After the war, the Kernel went unhappily back to his old job at the Commerce and Industry Association. He had reveled in the problems of wartime military government. When he was offered a chance to help the Japanese revamp their erratic tax structure, he took it and was sent out as a fiscal authority. Anne's mother followed shortly afterward, and from 1950 until the outbreak of the Korean War in 1952, the two were happily engrossed in the Japanese culture and its revitalization.

When the war in Korea broke out in 1952, the Kernel had finished restructuring the Japanese taxation system. He waived his disabilities to volunteer his services as chief of the finance division for UNCACK

Anne pregnant with Alec, 1952

The Kernel in Tokyo, 1951

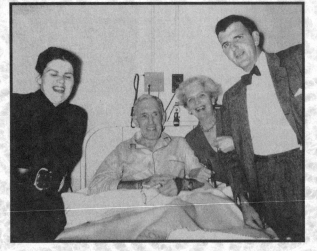

The family visits the Kernel in hospital

Alec Johnson, age 3

forces in Pusan. He enjoyed the job immensely and spared no efforts in doing the very best he could.

But, as in World War Two, the work taxed him horribly. In 1953, Anne received the shocking news that the Kernel had been sent back to Hawaii for a prostate operation. So she constructed a cheering telegram:

PROUD PROGENY PLEASED PERFECT PAPA POSTOPERATIVELY PROS-PERING. PLEASE PERPETUATE . . .

Not to be outdone, particularly when recuperating in a ward full of bored colonels and generals, the Kernel and his wardmates composed this reply:

PATERNAL PARENT POSITIVELY PURRING PLEASURE PAST PERFOR-MANCE PROMPTED PAEAN PRAISE PER PROGENY. PROSPECTS PROMISE PLUS PERADVENTURE. PRESENTLY PEEING PERFECTLY.

His message was held up for three days because the Army censors thought it was a code.

Back on the job, the Kernel continued to work long, hard hours. He felt it was the least he could do, given what the soldiers on the front lines were going through. But a man of sixty-two, who had survived two world wars, multiple coronaries, and diabetes, ran a severe risk trying to live as hard as twenty-year-olds. The Kernel contracted tuberculosis in 1953.

He was sent back to the States, to Castlepoint Veterans' Hospital in upstate New York. Anne went to visit him—and realized that he would never leave the hospital alive. He died quietly on January 25, 1954, before he had a chance to read that day's *Times*.

Soldier, citizen, patriot.

*J*ust after her return from Germany in the summer of 1963, Anne looked away from the depression of her musical letdown for a new horizon. She returned to science fiction and discovered science fiction conventions. She had heard of them from the writers at Milford, of course, but had never been to one. There was a big one that year in Washington, DC—just a few hours down the road by car.

A science fiction convention in those days was usually no more than a few hundred die-hard science fiction readers and writers who collected at a hotel for a weekend, sometimes a long weekend. There, the fans and the writers would talk about science fiction in the bar, or the fans would listen to various panels on science fiction by writers or other fans. And there, Anne could rub shoulders with writers she'd admired all her life: Isaac Asimov, James Blish, H. Beam Piper, Randall Garrett, and Keith Laumer.

Isaac was a charming genius, great at puns, limericks, and ditties—in addition to writing some of the finest popular science and school textbooks of this century—*and* a science fiction writer to boot. Even though he was a tenor (after her disaster in Germany, Anne would always say, "Never trust a tenor!"), he and Anne got along famously. Years later, a panel with Isaac and Anne on it would be the high point of many science fiction conventions, and fans would be in stitches from their raucous displays of barbed good humor.

But Anne was overcome more by James Blish's simple words of encouragement than by Isaac's humor. She found him and Evvie del Rey in the hotel bar where they were chatting between panels. The two greeted her warmly, though they had known her only casually before.

Then Jim said, "Anne, what has happened? You've published two *lovely* stories. What's happened? Why haven't you written anything more?"

"Well, I'm *trying* to."

"Well, you should continue."

And all the way home in the car Anne kept thinking to herself, "Jim Blish says I can write. Jim *Blish* says I can write. Jim Blish says *I* can write!"

And because Jim Blish said Anne could write, she did. Her next piece, "The Ship Who Mourned," was the first story of hers accepted by John Campbell at *Analog*.

Unlike Killashandra Ree of *The Crystal Singer*, Anne had sweet revenge. When she returned to the States she discovered that all that concentration on her lower range had actually shot her higher notes up to the E above high C and she continued to sing as a soprano, although the flaw in the lower E, F, and G remained.

Her vocal tutor, who had left Germany in search of a career in the States, came to her house one day when she was singing along with the radio and burst in, demanding: "Who is that marvelous soprano?"

"Me," Anne told him. But she had had enough of him and went back to her friend, choral master Ted Huang at the Concord Presbyterian Church. And Robie.

Anne with me

Anne also returned to the Breck's Mills Cronies for many more shows in various roles and off-stage positions. I remember the first time that I went to one of her performances. She was playing the wicked Queen Agravaine in *Once Upon a Mattress*. I must have been about eight at the time. She was so convincingly evil on stage—and it was a small theater with an intimate stage—that I got so terrified that she had to come out between acts to reassure me.

Anne started something new upon her return from Germany. We had all become so spoiled by the lovely fresh bread the Germans made that the thought of store-bought bread was too much, so Anne started making her own. Very soon, we were the most popular house in the neighborhood—particularly when the smell of warm, luscious fresh-baked bread wafted into the air. A good cook, Anne gained a divine reputation with her marvelous butter-basted loaves. We all got quite good at slicing thick warm bread and lathering it with butter and honey.

But Anne's famous home-baked bread became a thing of the past when the family teased her unmercifully after she tried to serve us from loaves she'd forgot to put yeast in. We called it "Lead Bread" and laughed at the idea of serving it to our neighbors and having them sink to the bottom of their bathtubs. Three decades wiser, I can only shake my head in memory and wistfully recall the smell of that marvelous fresh bread.

Fortunately, we learned from our mistake. And, as it turned out, our mother was far more willing to recognize her fallibility than our father would his. Wright decided that mustard soup was a brilliant idea; he refused to take "no" for an answer and we were all forced to finish off the ghastly stuff over the course of days. All in all, though, both my parents were excellent cooks and their rare culinary disasters were all the more memorable because they were so unusual.

The summer we returned from Germany, we saved up enough Green Stamps (anyone remember them?) to buy a hand-cranked ice cream maker. The ice cream was a bigger success than Anne's homemade bread. Our favorite was peach ice cream with just a hint of rose extract. Heaven. We would mix all the ingredients in the kitchen, carry the container out through the garage door, fill up the ice bucket with ice and salt, and turn that crank until we were breathless. That ice cream never survived long enough to get into the freezer.

Anne could turn out a good dinner from the time she was twelve, when she had made a planked steak with mashed potatoes and lemon meringue pie for dessert for her older brother and his date. She loved to cook.

Wright loved to entertain and was proud to have a wife who could prepare a dinner party. Cocktails would be served with hors d'oeuvres, dinner would follow after, and all throughout would be laughter, merriment, and good times. A talented wife, three kids, a car, a nice house; it was the American (male's) dream.

ife in Wilmington was not perfect. There were the occasional curve balls. Or loaded pistols. Windybush, the neighborhood we lived in, had been built by Mr. Eberhardt, an old, rich man who set himself up in one of the nicer houses. He had weak eyesight and strong opinions, particularly when it came to his cats.

Our German shepherd, Merlin—Wiz's son—would always follow the postman on his route to ensure that no other dogs bothered him. It was traditional, and no one ever minded because most everyone knew Merlin.

Unfortunately, Mr. Eberhardt decided that Merlin's purpose in life was to torment his cats. Despite all our best efforts, Merlin couldn't be dissuaded from following the postman, and Mr. Eberhardt wouldn't believe that Merlin, who had been raised as a puppy with three cats, wasn't the dog who chased his cats.

The situation came to a head one day when Mr. Eberhardt decided to take the law into his own hands and met Merlin and the postman at the door with a loaded pistol. Elderly, and with poor eyesight, he had the pistol pointing at the postman, not the dog.

Once Anne and Wright heard of the incident, they made an immediate decision: no matter the injustice of it all, Merlin would have to go. It was heart-wrenching for us kids, particularly for Alec and me, who were old enough to understand what was happening.

As a replacement guaranteed not to scare cantankerous old men into brandishing pistols, Wright got an apricot-colored miniature French poodle whom he named Michelangelo. We all promptly shortened it to "Angelo" and sometimes even "Angie." Now, to my mind, a miniature poodle is no replacement for a German shepherd. But Angelo was a friendly fellow, and Gigi decided that he was hers, as Alec and I had previously been the "owners" of the shepherds.

In 1965, Wright's job with Du Pont moved up to New York City. As a commute would have been impossible, the family chose to move. Decent housing in the Greater New York area was unaffordable. Fortunately, Wright's assistant, Jack Isbell, was faced with the same move and the same problems. They decided to pool their resources together and found an old three-story Victorian in Sea Cliff,

Long Island. Because communal living was not yet socially acceptable, we children were told that the Isbells were third cousins.

The house was conveniently located almost in the exact center of the triangle formed by the Franklin Elementary School, North Shore Junior High School, and North Shore High School. Gigi started first grade that fall, while I was entering third grade and Alec was in junior high.

Anne soon found that the amateur theater group in the area was more concerned about appearances and politics than with having fun, so after playing the Eve Arden role in *Babes in the Woods*, which she got because she could hold a B-flat for fifteen measures, Anne gave up amateur theater for good.

With the kids in school and nothing else to pique her interest, Anne resumed her writing, with gusto. That year she wrote and sold two more Helva stories and started work on what would become her first published novel, *Restoree*. *Restoree* was Anne's earliest blow for women's rights in science fiction. "I was so *tired* of all the weak women screaming in the corner while their boyfriends were beating off the aliens. I wouldn't have been—I'd've been in there swinging with something or kicking them as hard as I could."

Meanwhile Wright worked his way into his new job at Du Pont. Being back in New York was very attractive to him, particularly as his job involved him in various modeling spots. He got a shoot for Alec and lined up one for Gigi. This glamorous side of public relations appealed to him greatly. He liked mixing with the rich and famous, and was thrilled when the job connected him with a real Galitzine princess.

The evening commute was a frustrating hour or more by car or train. Back home, he enjoyed relaxing on the veranda before dinner, sipping martinis with his wife and the Isbells. As the stress of New York working—commute *and* office grind—increased, the cocktails before dinner got more frequent, becoming a daily ritual that grew from a single drink or two to a full pitcher or more. It became harder for Wright, trying to rebound from a day consulting with princesses, to communicate with a wife who very often was literarily on another planet.

Wright started blaming not Anne's writing, but her choice of genre for the gulf that grew between them, and held it responsible for the great change from their Wilmington lifestyle, forgetting that he had changed, that the children were growing, and that America itself had irrevocably awoken from the old Eisenhower-era American Dream.

Anne blamed the friction on Wright's drinking, and in a series of heated discussions got him to switch from martinis to wine. Wright responded by harassing her for writing science fiction. When Anne said that her writing helped to pay the bills, Wright replied, "Your writing will never pay the phone bill!"

Anne kept on writing. Wright took to buying wine in gallon bottles.

When it was completed, Virginia sent *Restoree* to Betty Ballantine at Ballantine Books. Betty bought it immediately. When I asked Betty what she remembers about reading *Restoree*, she said, "What I remember is the thrill that keeps editors going—when they first read something that says HERE IS A *WRITER!*"

Anne finished *Restoree* and "Weyr Search" before the summer of 1967. As the heat and humidity on Long Island grew more oppressive—particularly for those without air-conditioning—the family longed for a cool vacation, like the ones they had taken together in 1964 and again in 1966.

Back then, they settled on a large lodge at the Twin Lakes in the Poconos. The Twin Lakes were segregated—motorboat and sail—and we were on the larger, nonmotor side. The lodge was a huge wooden affair with rooms for everyone, and a good-sized kitchen. It had been the assembly hall of a summer camp.

The lodge came with its own canoe and rowboat. Down a path from the lodge was a short pier where the two boats were moored. I claimed the rowboat for my own most days and just doodled around in it on the lake.

In the evenings we'd build puzzles, big ones of 1,000, 1,500, and even 2,000 pieces. Some were in circles and were quite hard to build. Sometimes we'd play cards.

But the best thing about our times at the Twin Lakes were the blueberries. They grew wild on bushes where the lakes were joined and we'd row or canoe out there with buckets and fill them up with what we didn't eat.

Anne would rarely go on these trips as she was busy cooking most days, or writing when everyone was out and about. As a cook, Anne will always shine, but here, with fresh blueberries, she made the most marvelous blueberry pies you can imagine.

When we think of Pern's *bubbly pies*, we think of those fresh blueberry pies.

Back at our 1967 Sea Cliff home, Anne used the proceeds from *Restoree* to buy a Hermes Ambassador typewriter. She had encouraging news from John Campbell at *Analog*: he wanted more dragon stories. Anne wrote the story of Ramoth's growth into a full queen and Lessa's growth into a full dragonrider, the section known as "Dragonflight." But John Campbell said he wanted something different; he wanted to see dragons fighting Thread.

Anne, who had never done more than punch her elder brother out—he had a glass jaw—tried again and wrote the section "Crack Dust, Black Dust." John read it and said it was fine as far as it went. He gave her some suggestions on how to improve it.

Once more, Anne took over the living room. And she thought over how John had said to do it. "But that isn't the way *I* would do it," she said. She puzzled it over, and remembered John Campbell's suggestion of time travel. And suddenly it all came together. *Dragonrider* was born.

John Campbell bought it and invited Anne in to New York City for lunch. He often invited several writers for lunch and would spin off ideas just to see what would come back. He was always very encouraging.

"In fact," says Anne, "it was his comment on the novelette 'Dragonflight'—'A very good bridger for your novel'—that made me realize I was writing a novel."

It *was* a good bridger, and it gave the novel its name: *Dragonflight*. Betty Ballantine, who already had another contract with Anne for *Decision at Doona*, gladly bought it.

I've already mentioned that Anne wrote *Decision at Doona* with her younger son—me—in mind. Anne's ideas for her books did not all start in the front room at Sea Cliff. *Decision at Doona* was conceived in the Franklin Elementary School auditorium. It started when Anne heard that I was the only child the teachers had to tell to be quieter rather than louder when acting in our fourth-grade play.

Hearing this, Anne asked herself what would happen if you had a very compact society, an overcrowded planet, where just talking too loudly made you a social outcast? And that's how *Decision at Doona* was born.

"May you get what you wish for" is one of the three great Chinese curses. Anne fell afoul of it with me and my voice. She spent nearly twenty years saying, "*Lower* your voice," and when I finally learned how—her hearing went. And now it's, "Speak up, I can't hear you."

Every book is written differently. The author is the one who gets the words on paper. Very often, the editor helps the writer get the *right* words on paper. John Campbell helped Anne get the right words for "Weyr Search" and "Dragonrider."

With *Decision at Doona*, Betty had Anne rewrite the last third of the novel. She had asked Anne to rewrite only two scenes in her first book, *Restoree*. No changes were needed for *Dragonflight*.

The relationship between a writer and a publisher or editor is complex. Betty Ballantine says, "The editor/author relationship is

Betty Ballantine and Anne

second only to marriage. Any publisher worthy of the name needs also to be a psychiatrist, banker, lawyer, and—above all—friend strong enough to withstand some knockdown, drag-out fights. Not that *that* ever happened with Anne."

Betty liked *Dragonflight*. She liked it enough to sign a contract for its sequel before a single word was written. Writing *Dragonquest* would prove to be a great trial for Anne and a huge triumph for the editor/author relationship.

Anne was never working on just *one* story at a time. While she was writing the stories that would become *Dragonflight*, she hadn't forgotten about "The Ship Who Sang" and wrote several more stories in that universe. And a different story, the one that she had submitted to Milford at the same time she gave Virginia the unfinished *Weyr Search* to read, was polished up and sold as "A Womanly Talent."

I remember once back in her study when she showed me a slide; it was a picture of a spaceship floating on an ocean. *Galaxy Science Fiction* magazine had bought the art for a cover, and Judy-Lynn Benjamin was tasked with finding someone to write the story to match the picture. Anne tried and tried with that one and finally came up with a story to match the painting: "The Weather on Welladay." It was the first time Anne and Judy-Lynn worked together as author/editor, and it was a rewarding experience for both of them.

When the check for *Restoree* came in from Ballantine, Anne put paid to Wright's taunt about paying the phone bill. She not only paid it but bought him the sailboat he'd been ogling. He stopped taunting her about the money, but not about the writing. For him, science fiction was not "real" literature, not the sort he could brag about to his business contacts.

Only once did he and Anne connect over her writing, when she showed him the early draft of "Dramatic Mission," one of the stories in *The Ship Who Sang*. Wright was really impressed; he felt that it should be a novel and that she should have gone into the psychological trauma the people were having. The disagreement grew so great that I was dragged into it. I can't remember who asked me, but I do recall reading that draft. I was only twelve or so; as a twelve-year-old I thought the story was boring and was not convinced that exploring the psychological trauma wouldn't make the story more boring—but it might not. In the end, Anne told Wright that if he wanted to write a novel like that, he should go ahead, but it was not the story *she* was telling. It was the last time that Anne tried to interest Wright in her work.

Anne was not incapable of taking criticism; her survival at Milford was solid proof of that. More evidence came when she finished her first draft of *Dragonquest*. *Dragonflight* had done very well, garnering such positive reactions that Anne could not help but feel that the sequel would have to be better. She worked hard to that end.

So when she sent the manuscript up to Virginia Kidd, she was in high spirits. Virginia read it carefully and said the two words agents only rarely say to authors and authors dread: "Burn it."

Anne did. "Virginia was absolutely right," she says now. "It was awful."

If the relationship between a writer and a publisher is complex, it is nothing compared to that of the relationship between a writer and an agent. The strength of the relationship, and the friendship, between Virginia and Anne has never been so evident as in Virginia's conviction that she could be so honest in her criticism, and that Anne could be so accepting.

While Virginia could often tell Anne where something went wrong and give her an idea of how wrong it was, she was not an editor.

After Anne had burned the original *Dragonquest*, she set the project aside and didn't return to it for six months. When she did, she started completely from scratch. She got all the way up to page 170 and the story stopped. "It just wouldn't write."

The contract for *Dragonquest* was with Ballantine Books. Betty knew that Anne was under a lot of stress, so she invited Anne up to the Ballantines' Bearsville home for the New Year's break in January 1970.

"Well," Anne says, "anyone may think that they've had their work taken apart bit by bit, phrase by phrase, but you haven't until you've had a topflight editor like Betty Ballantine *sitting* and making you explain, expatiate, and clarify everything you have written."

They were about halfway through that grueling process when Betty had an inspiration. "You know the trouble with this story is, it's not about Lessa and F'lar, it's about F'nor and Brekke."

And with those words, the frame was set. Back in Sea Cliff, Anne finished the novel in record time and sent to Betty. Betty said, "I like your idea about the white dragon."

Anne explained that the idea had come from another great science fiction writer, Andre Norton, who had said that Anne ought to have a sport dragon and he should be white and small. Betty agreed, and said that Anne ought to do more with the white dragon. And so they signed a contract for *The White Dragon* in the summer of 1970.

Neither of them thought for a moment that it would be nearly seven years before the book was delivered.

Notes on Dragonquest

Ian Ballantine

Andre Norton with Anne McCaffrey

The tension that beset Anne in 1970 came from a number of things, some good, some bad.

The Good:

In 1968, Anne felt that the writers in science fiction had given so much to her that now it was time for her to pass on the favor. She wanted to help new writers the same way she had been helped.

Back in 1965, to promote the interests of professional science fiction writers, Damon Knight had founded the Science Fiction Writers of America, or SFWA. All the prominent science fiction authors joined the new organization and it acquired great status in its efforts to help J. R. R. Tolkien get fair recompense in America for pirated sales of *The Lord of the Rings*.

Anne nominated herself for and won the position of Secretary-Treasurer. It was a two-year post.

It did not leave her much time for writing. She had to get out the monthly premiere *SFWA Bulletin* and the chatty *SFWA Forum*—particularly the *Forum*. As Secretary-Treasurer she inherited the old, cranky mimeograph machine. All too often, the fragile stencils would tear apart while the *Forum* was being printed and would have to be rewritten.

Once a month, Anne would collect the pages in the great downstairs dining room and rope in "volunteers" to collate them. Actually, it was a whole lot of fun because we had a huge table and we'd place the pages all around it—so you'd do this dance around the table, picking up a page and going on to the next until you came back to the beginning with a whole *Forum*.

At that time I'd managed to find a fellow science fiction reader in my school and often, he, my little sister Gigi, and I would be the ones to help Anne pull the *Forum* together. Sometimes, Anne would have help from the local science fiction writers, and there would be a large party atmosphere that made the work go very quickly.

It was before and after such collating parties that Anne entertained numerous young writers including Jack Dann, Gardner Dozois, Pamela Sargent, and Patrice Duvic.

Anne attended more science fiction conventions, in those days the lifeblood of science fiction. In 1968, science fiction was something that teachers didn't want you to read, that parents loathed, and that rarely occupied more than a handful of shelves at the local bookstore.

Many books achieved good sales through word of mouth—and the patience, dedication, and perseverance of the publisher. Science fiction conventions were where word of mouth worked best.

That was the year that Anne brought me to my first science fiction convention, a Lunacon in New York City. I remember seeing Harlan Ellison doing one-handed push-ups; talking with Isaac Asimov; and going out to dinner with Robert Silverberg. And I remember being entranced by Ian Ballantine's twinkling eyes and bushy eyebrows.

Every year there was one big convention: the World Science Fiction Convention, known as Worldcon. Like bees to honey, science fiction readers and writers alike would flock to the Worldcon. Not only was the atmosphere always electric—alive with readers and writers mixing together, swapping enthusiastic tales or exploring some new aspect of science—but also the Worldcon was the place where every year the fans awarded that year's best novel, novella, novelette, and short story with the Hugo, an award named after Hugo Gernsback, one of science fiction's early lights and great editors.

Shortly after it was founded, the Science Fiction Writers of America agreed that there should be similar awards voted yearly by its membership. Their award was called the Nebula—SFWA's version of Hollywood's Oscars. But, at the time, Hollywood had nothing like the Hugo, an award from the readers of the genre for what they considered to be the best in the field. (Now, of course, there are the People's Choice awards.)

Although just back from Europe with Gladdie, Anne got Wright to agree to let her attend the 1968 Worldcon, partly because her story "Weyr Search" had been nominated for the Hugo award.

The 1968 World Science Fiction Convention, Baycon, was held in Berkeley, California. There were student riots at the time. Betty and Ian Ballantine, who were staying at a different hotel from the main convention site, got teargassed on their way to the convention. Anne herself suffered a bit of culture shock, going from quaint England and Ireland to the modern San Francisco Bay area—even more from discord between the ever-polite Irish to the antiwar student rioters.

At the convention itself, Anne started to relax. She met David Gerrold, fresh from his success with the marvelous *Star Trek* episode, "The Trouble with Tribbles." The two hit it off immediately. When Anne mentioned that she was Secretary-Treasurer of SFWA, Dave asked, "Can I join SWFA?"

When Anne asked if he had any credentials, David said, just "The Trouble with Tribbles," did that count? and Anne replied, "Well, I'm Secretary-Treasurer and I say it does."

Anne had acquired a *Carabinieri* cloak from Wright's first trip to Milan for Du Pont, and it had become her signature at science fiction conventions. At one party at Baycon, it was used as a prop for whoever entered the room. The cloak was made of black wool with a red lining, and most people chose to be a vampire in the classic Dracula pose, while others would pretend to be the Scarlet Pimpernel. Robert Silverberg was the most ingenious. Upon donning the cloak, he dropped to his knees in front of Anne and proclaimed, "I'm sorry, your Majesty, but we've had to cancel the Royal Foxhunt. Thy spendthrift ways have bankrupt the nation!"

David and Anne discovered that they both had something nominated for a Hugo: Anne's "Weyr Search" and David's "The Trouble with Tribbles."

David lost. Anne won.

"I remember being so ecstatic I could have flown home without a plane. Gene [Roddenberry] and Majel [Barrett] were complimentary and sincerely so, and Ian and Betty were delighted. Dave didn't win, but he was as sweet as could be over losing. There were many parties that night, and I remember Phil K. Dick urging me to write as much as I could right now, and get the benefit of the award's publicity. He was very nice to me.

"I remember phoning home to tell everyone my good news and I think even Wright was impressed. Betty and Ian took my plane tickets and upgraded me to first class so I could sit with them."

The triumph of that occasion has never been paralleled. Anne Mc-Caffrey was the first woman to win a Hugo award for writing science fiction. With her Hugo, no one could deny that she was a serious writer of science fiction.

The Bad:

Some people had no trouble belittling science fiction writers, and others were still ignorant. "Now that we've landed on the Moon, just what'll y'all write about?" asked one society columnist assigned to cover a science fiction convention the year Buzz Aldrin and Neil Armstrong set foot on the Moon. Harlan Ellison took the lady away, kindly but firmly telling her to have her newspaper send over their *science* editor.

The landing on the Moon had not brought science fiction out of the closet and into social acceptance, nor raised it any higher in H. Wright Johnson's regard.

Higher in Wright's affections were gardening and sailing. Wright loved a beautiful garden, but he didn't like to weed. Fortunately for him, he had two growing sons who could do that little something to earn their keep. Unfortunately, Wright was never trained in the better styles of leadership—to put it mildly. So, while he was in the basement working with seedlings and sipping martinis, he expected his boys to be out in the hot, humid, Long Island summers gladly pulling up weeds for the greater glory of gardening. This division of labor might

Wright with Angel's Cloud

just have worked if Wright had not also insisted upon drafting the boys as waiters for his outdoor dinner parties and loudly boasting about how he did all the garden work himself.

When Anne funded Wright's purchase of the sailboat *Angel's Cloud*, a nineteen-foot skipjack Chesapeake Bay clammer, she might well have hoped that it would improve the relationship between sons and father, because they all had a love of sailing. But Wright's manner soon cast such a pall on sailing that he was hard-pressed to find a crew, and when the boat was swamped in a storm in the spring of 1970, he was the only one of the family who cared.

In 1968, Anne had been a staunch supporter of Robert Kennedy's bid for the presidency. She felt his loss very deeply when he was assassinated, since she had known him at college. Then, in 1970, her eldest son, Alec, had to worry about his "lottery number" for the draft—it was the height of the Vietnam War—and ponder whether he would flee to Canada or accept service if worse came to worst.

Inside and out, Anne's family was battered.

The Good again, with a twist:

The Secretary-Treasurer of SFWA had many responsibilities. One of the more enjoyable jobs was helping in the construction of the Nebula awards. These were made from a lucite block encasing a disk-like galaxy spinning above a quartz crystal. Anne thought it would be fun for us kids to help make the Nebula galaxies. The Nebula galaxies were made by taking a clear lucite disk, putting spirals of glue on the top and sides, sprinkling silver sparkles on the glue, blowing off the excess and—voilà!—a Nebula galaxy.

It was not as much fun at the time as it is looking back over all those years and realizing who got those Nebula awards. Maybe Anne planned it that way.

You see, one of the other responsibilities of the Secretary-Treasurer is handing out the Nebula awards at the Nebula banquet. And that meant getting the Nebulas engraved with the right names *before* the awards banquet. So, as Secretary-Treasurer, Anne was one of the very few people who knew the winners ahead of time.

Which was okay with her. Except that in 1968, "Dragonrider" had been nominated in the Best Novella category. And it won—which meant that Anne would be the first Secretary-Treasurer to have the rather awkward honor of presenting herself with an award. So she did what any wise science fiction author does in such circumstances: she chickened out.

She called Isaac Asimov. They had been friends for over six years and he lived in New York.

"Isaac, I need a favor," Anne said.

"For you, Anne, anything," he said. She explained the problem to him.

"No problem, Anne, I would be delighted to present you with the award," Isaac gallantly responded. "But I would like to say a few words first."

Now I should warn you that Isaac Asimov was an accomplished tenor, raconteur, punster par excellence, as well as an incredibly bright, friendly, and talented person. All of which *should* have been for the best.

At the banquet, a nervous Anne handed over the podium to Isaac to present the award for Best Novelette. Isaac thanked her. He then started into a lengthy discussion of music, musicals, and his favorite songs. This discussion turned into a monologue on names and how they lent themselves to song. Isaac illustrated this by picking many famous science fiction writers' names and putting them to popular songs.

"Which brings me to the recipient of this award," Isaac finished. "The recipient has such a mellifluous name that only the very best of songs could possibly fit it." He paused, and added dramatically, "I suppose you are all familiar with the tune of 'San Francisco.' "

And, in his best Al Jolson imitation, Isaac belted out,

"Anne Mc-Caf-frey,

open your golden gates!

I can no longer wait!"

Red with embarrassment, eyes brimming with tears of laughter, Anne leaped up from her seat and, as she made her way to accept the award, joked to the room, "Never trust a tenor! Isaac, I'll get you for this!"

And she did.

She had her opportunity a lot sooner than she expected—at Boskone, the local Boston science fiction convention, about three weeks later. Isaac had been asked to give the E. E. "Doc" Smith

Isaac Asimov poses

Award. Naturally, the occasion allowed him to make a few more remarks. He was then going through a painful divorce and was nervous and depressed. His initial statement to the crowd went like this,

"I am always happy to give awards, though I'd be happier to receive some myself. Right now, among all my societies, it is you—and science fiction—whose good opinion I require. I want you to love me, love me, love me, or I will die."

With a sudden burst of joy, Anne shouted from the back of the room, "Live, Tinker Bell!"

Through the laughter, Isaac shook his finger at her. "Five minutes alone with you and I'll prove that I'm no Tinker Bell!"

Which, of course, got even more laughs.

Anne says, "I can't remember now—though Isaac would, God rest the man—when we started our traditional duet of 'When Irish Eyes Are Smiling.' It would have been at one of the New York City or Boston cons, but it became a feature. We were goaded to sing together at every convention we attended.

"Isaac always tried to pitch it higher than I could sing, but I could hit, on my good days, E above high C. There was a rough transition that ruined my voice—as I mention in *Crystal Singer* and *Killashandra*—but 'Irish Eyes' was always lustily rendered whenever Isaac and I were together."

Like the poor sailboat, Anne's marriage was swamped by spring storms. Many factors made it rocky: the boys were teenagers, Anne's career was taking off, Wright's career was stalled. In the hot summers, bitter arguments broke out across the dinner table. Wright would retire early to his room to play classical music and drink wine, to the relief of the rest of the family.

Wright's ideas of discipline were typical for a child of the Depression—a belt, a shoe, a cane reed, and, only as a last resort, the back of his hand. As teenagers after the "Summer of Love," we found none of those methods to be welcome or effective.

The defining moment for Anne was different than the defining moment for me. Anne remembers talking to me one night. She recalls that I said, "I know why Dad hits me so much: Alec would hit him back, and he'd leave marks on Gigi's face."

I remember one night when we were all at the kitchen table after dinner, drinking coffee. Dad and Mum were bickering back and forth, facing each other across the table. He was nagging her to write a letter, which she said she'd do when she had finished her coffee. He kept nagging. She threw the dregs of her coffee at him. He responded by throwing the last of his coffee in her face. Alec and I started up from the table, but Mum waved us back down. "That didn't hurt," she said. Then Wright threw the empty cup at her face.

This time Alec and I were on our feet before Mum could say anything. It didn't matter who did something like that; it was too much. It was Alec who told Dad he had better leave.

Not long after that, Wright moved out. In August, two years after coming back from her first trip to Ireland, Anne flew down to Tijuana and filed for divorce.

In 1970, divorce was still considered uncommon and uncouth. After Wright left, Peggy Isbell asked Anne to leave the huge house in Sea Cliff when the school year was over. So Anne had to deal not only with the legal and social tangles of divorce, but with the prospect of having nowhere to live.

Wright suggested that Anne move down to Princeton, New Jersey, where the school system was known to be good. He was an alumnus of Princeton University.

That didn't happen. Irish eyes were smiling. The Irish *Taoiseach* or prime minister, Charles Haughey, had just passed in 1969 a bill making resident artists and writers exempt from Irish taxes.

Harry Harrison, a science fiction writer who would soon have one of his books made into the film *Soylent Green*, took residence in Ireland and was happy to extol its virtues. At the time the price of food, clothing, and housing were half the US price.

Anne checked her finances. She couldn't make it, even with the contract for *The White Dragon* from Ballantine and the steady trickle of royalties from her three books. She was just about a book contract short. Magically, Betty Ballantine realized that Ballantine Books would be happy to publish a collection of recipes from science fiction authors—and would Anne be willing to edit such a book? Anne, who loved to cook and had a large supply of her own recipes, was thrilled and *Cooking Out of This World* was born.

So in August 1970, divorced, Anne handed over the post of SFWA Secretary-Treasurer to Roger Zelazny and packed to leave her home of five years and her country of birth. Gigi and I were coming with her; Alec, who was starting college, would remain behind.

Because of the lengthy (and expensive) six-month quarantine period, it was decided—with great difficulty and heavy hearts all around—that none of the family pets would come to Ireland. Ever since our original three cats in Wilmington, we'd had an orange marmalade born and raised at home. The current one, Maxwell Smart, was not the best representative. Alec took him to Stony Brook University. Unfortunately, Maxwell, lacking in brains, did not recognize his good fortune and escaped, never to be seen again. (I think his defection broke Alec's heart.) Wright took the other two cats, Tasso and Silkie Blackington, and the family's French poodle, Angelo.

Labor Day weekend is the traditional time for a Worldcon, but in 1970, as with every fourth year, the Worldcon was held outside North America—this time in Heidelberg. However, whenever the Worldcon is outside North America, a secondary convention—the North American Science Fiction Convention, or NASFiC—is held. In this case, the NASFiC convened in Toronto. Anne was invited as co–guest

Alec Johnson

Anne and Isaac. "Never trust a tenor!"

of honor with Isaac Asimov. Happily, the convention paid her way to Toronto. And it was cheaper to go to Ireland by way of Toronto.

It certainly was more heartening. Isaac Asimov and Anne had a great time trading "insults" to the delight of the con-goers, singing duets, and generally having a marvelous time.

Anne's arrival in Ireland did not begin auspiciously. Gigi got terribly sick, maybe with food poisoning, and Anne's arm was ruined from lugging her heavy IBM Selectric typewriter and three other pieces of hand luggage through the airport to the airplane. The plane was supposed to stop in Shannon and fly on to Dublin. But Dublin was socked in with fog, and Shannon only barely less so. We deplaned and waited for hours in the arrivals lounge while the airline figured out what to do.

Anne's first trip to Ireland had been much more pleasant, and the plane had gone straight on to Dublin. Perhaps it was wishful thinking, or maybe just pure luck, but at that very moment she spotted Pat Brown, her chauffeur from her first trip. Pat was delighted to see her and pointed the airport nurse her way before reluctantly taking his own party on their tour. With some ginger ale, Gigi's stomach became less queasy, but she was still very ill. The airline finally ascertained that there would be no break in the weather at Dublin and so decided to bus all the Dublin passengers to the Shannon train station and then transport them up to Dublin by train.

In all, what would have taken forty minutes by air, took over seven hours. We arrived at Heuston station late that night in fog and light rain and took a taxi to our hotel.

The diminished family spent the next couple of days recovering. The Royal Marine Hotel in Dun Laoghaire (pronounced "Dun Leery") was a warm, friendly place and the staff was quite convivial with the three "Yanks."

The Irish culture, particularly in Anglicized Dublin, has a strong overlay of English culture. Both are different from the cultures in the United States. Anne and the kids first realized this when they were served cold toast. At first they passed it off as a fluke, but as the days went by they decided that the distance to the kitchen was so great that the toast cooled before it was served. Finally they began to wonder if the rumors of lazy Irish were true, only to discover that the staff would not rush to serve them toast because it had to cool! It was then that they learned that in Ireland and England, it's considered impolite to serve hot toast.

I was very worried about going to Ireland. It was a tremendous jolt, moving from the States after the divorce. On top of that, all I had were the Hollywood images of Ireland. I was convinced that I would have to explain electricity and that we'd ride in carts all over the place. I was also terribly worried that they wouldn't have peanut butter, jelly, popcorn, or hot dogs.

Once I realized that a Mars bar was exactly like the American Milky Way bar, only better, and that I was paying two shillings—twenty-four cents—for what would cost thirty-five cents in the States, I became quite enamored of Ireland.

I soon also discovered that there was an "okay" peanut butter, that bramble jelly was an acceptable substitute for Concord grape jelly, and that they did have popcorn—although the Irish would sugar rather than salt it. Good hot dogs were hard to come by. But when I discovered Jelly Tots, I was quite willing to forgive Ireland that minor inconvenience.

While our stay at the Royal Marine was marvelous, it was costly. Anne undertook to get the family into cheaper accommodations before the school year began. So, armed with maps of Dublin city, she rented a car and took the kids house hunting.

The Irish and English drive on the left side of the road, opposite from Europe and the States. The reason for this is historical: Napoleon Bonaparte decided that his soldiers should march on the right—and as he conquered most of Europe, Europe was forced to follow suit. All this took place in the early 1800s, so the Americans followed the French because they were still mad at the English.

What it meant for Anne was that every time she went to shift gears she'd bang her right hand against the door until she remembered that the gear shift was on the *left*. It also meant that driving required intense concentration. As the eldest child present, I took on the role of map-reader and navigator, which took that strain from her, and she was very gracious about the times I got us lost.

As we looked at houses for rent, we experienced another culture shock. Houses and the lands surrounding them were much smaller in Dublin than back on Long Island. While the rents were incredibly cheap by American standards, the rooms were pretty small; the kitchens were like closets.

We ended up choosing a semi-detached house in upscale Mount Merrion on 14 North Avenue. Settling in, Anne finished *Dragonquest* and sent it off to Ballantine to be published in 1971. She also finished two gothics—*The Mark of Merlin,* reusing a plot she'd set up in her freshman college year, and *Ring of Fear.*

Anne's mother arrived when the family had set up in 14 North Avenue. She had wanted to retire from her real estate job, and Anne's relocation to Ireland had given her an added impetus. She was in her seventies, and found Irish weather a bit colder than she would have liked. But "Bami"—as we kids called her—was a welcome addition to the household.

Another welcome addition was our orange marmalade cat, the first family pet in Ireland. We named him Isaac Asimov—and then realized that he had to be neutered, allowing Anne to later joke in the family that she had had Isaac Asimov fixed. The real Isaac was informed of the cat's name and approved, but we never informed him of the "snippery" (of which he probably *wouldn't* have approved).

ack at the Royal Marine Hotel, in the evenings Anne would venture out to the local pubs, leaving the kids asleep or under the friendly eyes of the hotel staff. At a furniture store, Anne had met Michael "Mick" O'Shea. "You sound like a Yank," Mick had said. "What part do you hail from?" Afterward, they met at the Eagle House, just up the street from the hotel.

14 North Avenue

Annett Francis, whom Wright
married in 1970

Isaac Cat

Mick introduced Anne to a wild group, some Irish, some English. There was Dominic and his girlfriend, Mick's girlfriend Ann, and Bernard Shattuck, a soft-spoken Englishman who was a first mate on a trawler, working for his captaincy. Mick himself—a six-foot, red-haired, red-bearded giant—claimed to have been in the Royal Marines and the Royal Air Force, both. He ran a car-repair shop and helped Anne find an old black Morris four-door sedan.

Equipped with a car, we all went roving on the weekends. Anne found a local stables, Dudgeon's, and found that she could indulge herself and the children in riding lessons. Anne's first instructor was a young American, Mare Laben. Mare had come over to study horsemanship at Dudgeon's. They became good friends and much later, when Mare needed a place to stay, Anne invited her to stay with us.

nne had given David Gerrold an open invitation to come stay with us if he ever decided to investigate Ireland. David gladly accepted and arrived before Christmas. Unexpectedly, Anne's mother took a tremendous and surprising dislike to David. However, there was no way to overcome it. To spare Anne any distress, David decided to move out and rent an apartment.

Mick O'Shea came to the rescue; he knew an apartment that was open two houses down from his.

The next day David phoned Anne. "Lessa is my landlord," he told her.

"What do you mean?"

"Lessa is my landlord," David repeated. "You have to meet her."

At five-foot-nothing, and ninety pounds sopping wet, the brown-eyed, black-haired Jan Regan had all the feistiness, self-determination, and strength of Lessa of Pern. There being no dragons available, Jan had contented herself with exercising racehorses. More than twenty years later, Jan is still a close friend of the family.

*A*nne had not quite recovered from the shock of her mother's behavior toward David when she got another shock: the announcement from Wright that he was exercising his option to visit the children. He would come in the spring and bring his new wife.

Gigi and I were stunned. We had known nothing about Wright's romantic involvement, and were unprepared to see our father with a new wife.

Anne was amused to note that Wright's new wife was only eleven days younger than herself—and her name was Annett! Annett Francis was an editor with *House and Garden*.

The visit was a disaster. Wright's attitude toward his ex-wife irritated us, and his insistence that Gigi and I unequivocally accept his new wife turned the visit into a nightmare for everyone. Annett and Anne both desperately tried to smooth out the visit—they got along together very well—but their efforts could not counteract Wright's behavior.

The visit left a pall that hung over the household. To break it, and to make her entrance into British fandom, Anne planned to bring us with her to the annual British Easter convention. That year it was held in Worcester, which is pronounced "Wooster," and the convention was called Woostercon.

We took the car and crossed the Irish Sea by ferry to Liverpool. Dave Gerrold came, too. It was a magical trip. The British fans and writers were magnificent and made us all feel very welcome. Anne had a marvelous time on panels with Brian Aldiss, Bob Shaw, and James White. I was introduced simultaneously to *The Hobbit* and Dungeons and Dragons.

Many new lifelong friends were made at that first British convention. Dr. Jack Cohen was one of the most memorable. Jack holds a doctorate in Science in reproductive biology and had just started

Dr. Jack Cohen

working on a male contraceptive pill. He also gave the most hilarious lectures—with slides—on reproductive biology. When Anne met him, he was on the verge of getting married. Anne invited him and his intended, Judy, to come to Ireland whenever they wanted.

With the convention over, Anne planned an itinerary winding through Wales to the southern ferry port of Fishguard. The first stop was Stonehenge, the most famous and one of the oldest rings of standing stones in the British Isles. In those days Stonehenge was just coming to be respected as a significant historical artifact. Visitors were allowed to wander freely on the site and through the stones. It was awe-inspiring.

About seventeen miles outside of Fishguard, on the narrow curving hill road, we heard a noise from the front wheel on the passenger's side of our car. The twisting roads through Wales had taken more time to cover than Anne had planned and there was a very real danger of missing the ferry, so Anne braved onward, in spite of my pleas to pull over.

We made the ferry with only minutes to spare, but I made my mother promise to have the wheel checked at the first garage—service station—we found back in Ireland. When the mechanic took off the hubcap, we could see all the tire nuts firmly in place. I felt rather foolish, until he pointed to the hub nut sitting in the hubcap! The whole front wheel, hub and all, had been held on only by the caliper brakes the entire way through the winding hills of Wales!

Not long after, the Morris died completely. While Anne was searching for a replacement, Mick loaned her any number of oddball cars. One of the oddest was a three-speed car that always had to be push-started, but most memorable was the two-seater MG Sprite. It made a decent two-seater, but was used as a family car, with the spare children lying on the spare tire behind the passenger. It was a lot of fun.

Anne wanted a horse. Anne had *always* wanted a horse, but finally she was in a country where she might actually be able to *afford* one. And she wanted to hunt. She found that the place to look for horses was in the *Irish Field*. And in early spring, she saw an ad for someone to ride a hunter for the rest of the season, a 16.2-hand, dapple-gray heavyweight hunter.

After a trial ride, Anne got in touch with the owner, Hilda Whitton, a sprightly horse trainer with silver hair. Hilda had bought Mr. Ed as a yearling and brought him on to be a heavyweight hunter. She wanted to find Mr. Ed a proper home; she'd hurt her leg when she'd fallen after he'd been spooked by a JCB dumper (not quite the Irish equivalent of a bulldozer, but just as noisy) and at her age would never survive another bad fall.

Somehow a deal was struck and Mr. Ed went home with Anne. She stabled him at a private stable in Stepaside, but she really wanted him just outside her door. Then, as fall approached and she had to find a new rental, Anne got her wish in the most spectacular fashion: a 230-year-old Georgian mansion on two acres. It even had an old barn where a stable could be fitted.

Mr. Ed with Todd

Meadowbrook House was an amazingly good piece of luck. So good that, almost in recompense, Anne's luck dried up right after she signed the lease. Worse, so did her writing. She spent days staring at blank pieces of paper. Her gothic novel *The Year of the Lucy* was not accepted by her editor at Dell, and the expected payment was not forthcoming. Money got very tight.

Anne became very good at cooking leftovers and leftover leftovers. Of course, Anne's leftovers would make a gourmet cook jealous. It was during this dry spell in writing that Anne completed *Cooking Out of This World*, including her excellent recipe for lamb stew and another for potato pancakes. At dinner one night, Gigi asked wistfully, "Gee, Mom, wouldn't it be nice to have pancakes because we *wanted* them for a change?"

Relief came in the form of Anne's elder son, Alec. Alec had done poorly at Stony Brook and had not been invited back, so he joined us in Ireland. Bernard Shattuck introduced Alec to several trawler skippers and one was sufficiently impressed to give him a try. When Alec didn't "toss his cookies" in the fiercest gales Ireland had seen in twenty years, the skipper decided that maybe he'd do. The money and the odd fish kept the wolf from the door.

Virginia Kidd was aware of the tight finances and did what she could. When she heard that Roger Elwood was looking for young-adult stories, she told Anne, who spent hours wracking her head for inspiration. Finally she started a story about a young girl named Menolly . . . and it wouldn't go anywhere.

Anne gave up; another avenue blocked. Then she remembered her

Meadowbrook House

brother Kevin and how he had withstood all the pain and terror of his osteomyelitis, and the memory inspired her. In a few days she had finished and sent off "The Smallest Dragonboy," little realizing at the time that it would end up being the most reprinted story she had ever written.

The money from the sale was only $154, not enough to pay rent or tuition. Certainly not enough to pay for the cost of storing all the family's furniture and belongings left behind on Long Island. Anne talked it over with us, then tearfully wrote the warehouse telling them to sell off our goods.

The move to Meadowbrook House had not been without incident. Mick O'Shea and the whole crew had pitched in and helped with the move, but one of the cars they used had a faulty trunk, as they found out when its contents spilled out over the road. Our cat, Isaac Asimov, was another casualty. He got to Meadowbrook House, but he didn't stay long.

We quickly got a replacement cat. Alec had the honor of naming him "Zeke the Cork, Rabble-rowser from the Mountains" from Bob Dylan's book *Tarantula*. Zeke quickly grew to be a tall, lean, black-and-white cat with an unmatched sense of humor. Zeke's humor was pure cat; his favorite trick was jumping from the floor onto the top of an open door—a jump of over eight feet—and then quietly waiting until a suitably inattentive person passed underneath him. At which point he'd negligently comb that person's hair with his claws and greet their upturned faces with a "Why, whatever did I do?" smirk.

A stall was made in the barn in the backyard, and hay and straw were laid in for Mr. Ed. Zeke, living up to his name, had absolutely no fear of Ed. In fact, I remember being terrified the first night we were bedding Ed down. We'd put down a really nice thick layer of straw for Ed to sleep on, and into this walked Zeke. With a bound, he dove under the straw and was quickly lost from sight.

Ed was a marvelous horse with a keen sense of humor himself. This night he displayed it with what has to be one of horsekind's favorite practical jokes: He stepped on my foot and then—looking back at me with an "Is there something wrong?" look—he put his whole weight on that one foot! Frantically I pushed him off me; over sixteen hundred pounds of horse and only a hundred pounds of me.

So you can understand that with Ed in this mood, I was very worried for the safety of one very small and completely invisible young cat.

I need not have worried. Shortly after I got Ed off of my foot, he put his head down to the straw and blew gently over one spot. Out popped Zeke, trying very hard to pretend that he had *meant* for Ed to find him.

Anne shooed us all out and back to the house, leaving Ed and Zeke to get acquainted. When I came back the next morning, Ed was curled up on the ground. Horses are very nervous when they're lying on the ground—you rarely catch them there—so it was very odd. I was a bit worried until Ed cocked his head to look down at his chest.

There, between his legs, slept Zeke. Long after Anne had written the scene in *Dragonquest*, Ed and Zeke re-created the same sleeping arrangements that F'nor's brown Canth had with golden Grall.

The relationship between Ed and Zeke blossomed into something phenomenal. When the weather turned nice, Anne would let Ed out to graze on the front lawn. Meadowbrook House was surrounded by a high stone wall, but Ballinteer Road was a bus route. People on the upper deck of a double-decker bus could see into the front yard. It being Ireland, few would look askance at a horse grazing in the front yard. But we soon noticed that the bus riders were getting quite excited whenever Ed was out on a warm day. What they saw was that Ed had a very special helper warding off flies: Zeke the Cork, Flyswatter from the Hindquarters. Zeke would lie, paws up, on his back and swat the horseflies away. Every now and then Ed would tease him by swishing his tail or making an unexpected move. Once in a while, Ed would trick him—and there would be this very wide-eyed cat sliding down on his backside off Ed's rump. Even though it cost him his dignity, Zeke never once used his claws.

It is the nature of publishing that a book is finished at least a year before it gets published. While nearly a year had gone by since Anne had written *Dragonquest*, it was just now nearing publication. Betty Ballantine sent Anne a copy of the cover art as a courtesy. It happened on a day when the plumbing had gone bad again. Bernard

Shattuck and I were outside in the backyard running a plumbing snake—in this case a long line of bamboo poles that screwed together—in hopes of convincing the sewage to move into the septic tank rather than back to the house.

"Here, look at this," Anne said to Bernard with a smile. Bernard, a well-muscled young man with curly brown hair and soft brown eyes, looked at the cover and saw a well-muscled young man with curly brown hair and soft brown eyes perched on a dragon's tail.

"That's nice," he said. I looked at it over his shoulder, and at him, and back again. "That's *you*!" I said.

First we find Lessa in Jan Regan and then unbeknownst to us, an artist draws a F'nor that looks like Bernard Shattuck. Years later, Anne would remember Bernard directly by naming the captain of the *Mayflower*, in *Dragonsdawn*, after him.

E d—"Horseface," as Anne called him—was just a short walk from our kitchen door and always ready for a ride. While Anne did much of the mucking out of his stable and general grooming, we all took turns riding Ed.

I liked riding for enjoyment. Gigi was a more serious rider and often took Ed out for long rides. Poor Gigi came back in tears one afternoon, leading Ed. "He's hurt! He's hurt! He's bleeding! Help!" she shouted as soon as she got close.

Ed had cut a vein just above the ankle on a shard of glass. Gigi had

Mr. Ed and Zeke at
Meadowbrook House

Bernard Shattuck

done an excellent job of getting him back home as fast as she could without scaring him. The wound was spurting blood every time his heart beat.

Anne rushed out immediately with a kitchen towel. She cleaned the wound, located the cut, and pressed the wound shut with the towel wrapped around. Ed was worried and in pain. As soon as she felt he was stable and not shocky, she got me to take over while she went to phone the vet.

For the next hour we traded off, kneeling down by Ed and holding the vein closed while the kitchen towel got wetter and wetter, only to be replaced by a clean one, which in turn got drenched with blood. The backyard looked like a battle scene; the grass was smeared red with Ed's drying blood.

Finally the vet arrived. He took a while examining Ed, making sure of the extent of the wound and sizing up the options. "I'm going to have to anesthetize him," he said. We had to put a twitch on Ed—a rope that twisted his nose—to get him to stand still while the vet injected the anesthesia.

Ed fought the drug. When it finally took effect, he toppled slowly, nearly skinning his front knees before we could roll him onto his side. He lay there, legs straight out, eyes wide with fright, twitching. It was too much for Anne, who had been so calm throughout the ordeal. Before she lost it completely, I ran inside, found the liquor cabinet, and poured a shot of Cointreau. I rushed back and handed it to her. "Drink it."

It must have been the right thing to do, because Anne knocked it back, made a face, and said, "Thank you, I needed that."

The vet stitched up Ed, gave him the antidote for the anesthesia, and waited while the big horse got back on his feet.

The sun was setting as the vet told us, "He'll be all right. Just watch he doesn't cast himself." If a horse lies down against a wall it can position itself so that it can't get up again and the horse is "cast," a terrifying position for an animal and one that often results in horses thrashing themselves to death.

Anne sent off Gigi to make Ed's bed in the stable while we slowly walked him over. Gigi had laid a big deep pile of straw and Anne made him a rich mix of bran mash with an extra dollop of sweet molasses. Ed ate it hungrily. We all watched until we realized that he was all right and we were famished.

Ed's stable was just slightly out of line with the kitchen window, but not so much that we couldn't keep an eye on him. When Anne was cooking, one of us would watch out the window, and when she had to see for herself, one of us would stir the pot. I don't think we ate standing up, but I can't be sure.

It was late before we were willing to consider going to bed. Ed was still standing in his stall, pacing around in circles. He never did go to sleep; he was still on his feet the next morning, and the thick straw bed that had been laid for him had been ground into fine chaff.

*A*nne's mother was an amazing and well-loved grandmother. She taught me to play chess and was mature enough to play down at

Anne D. McCaffrey — "Bami"

Geoff Hilton

Barbara "Bals" Hilton, Gigi, and Anne
seated at the dining room table,
Meadowbrook House

my level, letting me win sometimes. By the time we were in Meadow-brook House, Bami had decided that I was old enough to play against her best and she would regularly trounce me. In fact, I don't remember beating her once when we were in Meadowbrook.

I had made friends with Geoff Hilton, a fellow schoolmate. Geoff's family was English; his father had been brought over by his company, Hoover. Aside from board games, mostly military war games, Geoff and I enjoyed playing chess, and I frequently beat the pants off of him. I learned later that Geoff would learn one new chess trick and beat me with it until I figured out on my own how to counter it.

I remember one day, however, when Bami was practically fuming that Geoff had trounced her with a new gambit that he'd thought up. Immediately afterward, she challenged me to a game. When I demurred, she nearly forced me to the chessboard. Well, she beat me in about five moves—I didn't know what had hit me.

Later, she was contrite. "I'm sorry, it's just that he *annoyed* me so!"

Geoff could be very annoying at the time. He occasionally "got my goat," but where he excelled was in tormenting his little sister, Babs. Barbara Hilton was Gigi's age and in Gigi's class, so they became good friends. Many weekends both Babs and Geoff would come over.

That worked out very well, with a few exceptions. The most memorable was at Thanksgiving dinner. Thanksgiving is a purely American tradition but one that Anne would never abandon. Anne's cornbread stuffing is the best in the universe—in my completely *un-biased* opinion, of course. She also made an excellent chestnut dressing, a great turkey gravy, magnificent mashed potatoes . . . I'm getting hungry just remembering the smells in Meadowbrook's small dining room that night.

It was delicious and after a long silence while the meal was eaten, everyone sat back, contented.

The moment was broken by a sniping exchange between Geoff and Babs. Whereupon Anne, attempting to recover the good mood, said, "But Geoff, we all know that the English only insult those they really love."

Geoff mulled this over for less than a second before turning to his sister, with a vicious twinkle in his eyes, and said, "Barbara, dear, have I told you how *marvelous* you look?"

While the sniping between Geoff and Babs was rare and got better with time, Anne was alarmed when she noticed that her mother had started snapping at the children and complaining all the time. Anne became convinced that it was just too hard to have three generations living in the same household and suggested that her mother consider taking an apartment.

In short order, Anne and her mother were in a vicious argument that ended with them not speaking to each other. After several days of tense silence in the house, Bami came to Anne one day and said, "I'm sorry I've been so mean. It's just that the children are too loud, everyone's too loud, and I've got this damned ringing in my ears."

It did not take long for Anne to realize that her stoic mother was in severe distress with a loud ringing in her ears: tinnitus. Bami's irritability only increased when we moved into our next house. Money had grown very tight, so we were forced to compromise and considered ourselves lucky to rent what we did—a semi-detached house in Dun Laoghaire on Rochestown Avenue, easy cycling distance from our school.

The road was a well-traveled one, complete with buses. There was no ancient wall to muffle the road noise. Very soon Bami could not stand it. The series of arguments erupted once more. One day Bami announced that she had found herself an apartment in Blackrock and no one could talk her out of moving. No one did. Within the week both Anne and Bami were thrilled with the new arrangement.

Bami's apartment was within walking distance of our school, and

Site 11,
Rochestown Avenue

while Gigi and I visited her often, she was more often entertaining her chess foe, Geoff Hilton. Years later Geoff would tell me how much he enjoyed his times with Bami and how jealous he was of me for my grandmother, but I think I am more envious of him for his friendship with her.

Bami had sailed the seven seas on tramp steamers after the Kernel had died, just for the pure fun of it all. She'd loved Japan when they'd been stationed there just after the war; she'd survived the Depression; she had a sharp wit, an acid tongue, and was . . . cool, formidable, a "caution." She was never far from a shot of Scotch, although she never drank excessively. In her travels she'd grown to love collecting ivory and sterling silver, and her apartment was adorned with beautiful oddments. She was a lady who had lived her life completely, had enjoyed it, and still enjoyed it.

In 1973 Anne had to take bank overdrafts between books to keep the family going. It was a lean year, both for writing and for income. It was rare for a woman to be a single parent and sole provider for her family in Ireland. Fortunately, Wright was still sending his child care payments, and, more fortunately, Betty and Ian Ballantine kept *Dragonflight*, *Dragonquest*, and all of Anne's other Ballantine books in print. The two dragon books had earned out their advance, so every new copy sold made money for Anne.

Anne still had to deliver on the Dell romance contract. Working with the old dictum "Write what you know," she started a book about the abuses against women that were rampant in Ireland and wrapped a strong, compelling story around it. The working title was *A Kilternan Legacy*, and it dealt with an American divorcée and two children trying to find their way in Ireland. The concept smacked of autobiography; the book was anything but.

Anne also started a series of connected novelettes for Roger El-wood, who had arranged a four-book series called *Continuum*. For *Continuum 1*, Anne wrote "Prelude to a Crystal Song," and continued on through the series with "Killashandra—Crystal Singer," "Milekey Mountain," and "Killashandra—Coda and Finale." When the series was completed, Anne pulled the four pieces together into one complete novel: *The Crystal Singer*. In *The Crystal Singer*, Anne was also writing from experience, using her past singing and subsequent disappointment as the basis for the story.

The big problem was Ed. Anne had to find a place to stable Ed and a way to pay for it. She wanted a stable nearby. The solution was Brennanstown Riding School, then located in nearby Cabinteely. The owner of the school was Jane Kennedy, a lean, spirited rider whose horse abilities were far greater than her people abilities. Jane attracted a few loyal supporters and many young helpers. At first Anne put Ed in on half livery—she paid half the cost of his keep, and he was ridden by pupils for the other half—but when she discovered that Jane needed help scheduling, running the accounts, and manning the phone, they came to an arrangement that lasted over six years.

On Saturdays, Anne—the award-winning science fiction writer—

would settle in at the office in Brennanstown to answer phones, make sure that students and teachers were assigned to horses, and manage the accounts. In some ways the juggling act was reminiscent of the times when Anne had been a stage director for the Breck's Mills Cronies.

Gigi, who was thoroughly horse-mad by then, would accompany her and gleefully muck out stables, feed and groom horses, clean tack, or cart hay for the pure joy of being in the proximity of a horse, and for the occasional free lesson. She was not alone in this and made friends with the other helpers. At that time there were Cliona, Eoiffa, Brenda, and Derval.

Poor Derval was always given a hard time whenever she went into the hayloft because of an unfortunate incident years back. She had been abstractedly piling out the hay near the entrance and, moving back to admire her handiwork, had stepped into the thin air behind the ladder. The ensuing fall broke her nose and both arms.

Derval took the slagging over this with the same cheerful good nature she showed at all times. Tall, a bit gawky, with an aquiline nose, full lips, curly hair, and an infectious smile, Derval was a character.

When, in 1974, Brennanstown had to find new stables, Jane Kennedy relocated the school to Kilmacanoque, just outside Bray—about ten miles farther away. To get the horses there, she enlisted all her helpers to hack the long distance. Gigi still remembers the marvelous time she had riding Ed and leading a string of ponies.

Derval Diamond

At the end of the school year, in the summer of 1973, when the lease came up on the Rochestown house, Anne was lucky to find a house close by available for a long lease. It was number 79 Shanganagh Vale in Cabinteely. The house was at the back of the development. It was a low bungalow, with three bedrooms, one bathroom, a long dining/living room, and a kitchen nearly as long. It was a lovely house and we all enjoyed its comfort for the next three years.

Nineteen-seventy-four was a tumultuous year for Anne, a roller-coaster year with more down than up. In the spring Wright was laid off by Du Pont. He informed her that as he had no income, he would no longer be able to pay child support. And in April, her elder brother's wife died after a long lingering bout with cancer.

On the upside, the New England Science Fiction Association, NESFA, asked her to be their guest of honor at their March 1975 convention, Boskone. A guest of honor had her airfare and hotel room paid for the convention. Anne gladly accepted. The invitation was made sweeter because NESFA had a tradition that the guest of honor would have a small press book published by NESFA Press and sold at the convention—and would she be willing to write a dragon story for them? The up-front fee was a welcome incentive. Anne was delighted. She arranged a signing tour with her publisher to start after the convention.

On the downside, I graduated from high school that year and wanted to go back to the States for college. I was accepted at Lehigh University, with a partial scholarship. Betty Ballantine graciously signed as surety on the tuition. Still, money was tight and I had to earn my own pocket money.

Alec was working in a garment-cleaning factory in Massachusetts and wrangled me a summer job. Gigi went to France for the summer on a foreign exchange program. Anne was alone for the first time in many years.

One of the few things that Anne always tried to have enough money for was a housecleaner to come in once a week. Anne did the cooking and the laundry, but the general cleaning she left to the housecleaner. The cleaning woman in Ireland was a sweet lady named Kathleen. When Bami had set up her apartment, she had asked Kathleen to come and clean for her, too.

Anne was alone in the house when Kathleen called her from Bami's. Kathleen had found Bami on the floor, unconscious. With quick thinking, she had remembered Bami's affinity for drink and had splashed a little bit of whiskey under her nose. Either the smell or the feel did the trick: Bami took a deep breath and continued breathing until the medics arrived.

The prognosis was not good: paralysis on the left side. Crippled, in a home, at best.

"She wouldn't have liked that," Anne recalls with tears in her eyes. "She always wanted to be active, to do things by herself. To have her just stuck in a shell . . . it wouldn't have been fair."

Those were bitter days, working at Brennanstown stable in the day, traveling to the hospital to sit with an unconscious mother, and being afraid of what the future would be for them both. After ten days with no change, Anne's mother had a second stroke on July 12 and passed away, never regaining consciousness.

Bami had requested that she be cremated. Cremations were not done in Ireland at the time. The coffin was shipped to Birmingham, England, for cremation, but Anne had no way to get herself there. Bereaved, newly orphaned, Anne was at a loss for what to do. Her Brennanstown friends helped her out. One of them, Simon Healy, was a pilot. Simon managed to get the loan of a plane, and flew Anne and Gigi over there just for the cost of the fuel. Simon's kindness, sympathy, and dedication made a very difficult journey as pleasant as possible.

Unfortunately, Anne couldn't afford to fly Alec and me over from the States. And now it saddened her that her mother, who had befriended so many people in her long life, had only a daughter and a granddaughter at her funeral.

For a long while Bami had spoken of having her ashes scattered in beautiful Galway Bay. While Anne plotted how to honor this request, Kathleen recounted how Bami had spoken often of resting in the family plot in Boston, next to her husband. So when the urn was brought to her later that month, Anne tucked it in the back of the family's Welsh dresser, next to her father's doctoral thesis, to wait until her tour of the States the next spring.

Gigi had not been feeling well since her return from France. Initially both she and Anne put it down to the stress of the moment. But when Gigi was still suffering after Bami's funeral, they sought medical advice.

Anne was again lucky in her connection with Brennanstown. Gigi's friends Anne and Orla Callaghan recommended their doctor, Hilary Webb. She quickly figured out that Gigi was suffering from more than normal stomach upsets and sent her on to the top gastroenterologist in Ireland, Dr. James Fennelly.

The news was bad: Gigi had Crohn's disease. To get to the diagnosis of Crohn's disease, both acute appendicitis and abdominal obstruction must be ruled out, which means that the symptoms are worse than both of these. Additional symptoms include severe colic, constipation, vomiting, malnutrition, chronic debility, and abdominal fistulas and abscesses often causing fever and generalized wasting. The worst of these symptoms were not yet manifest; all Gigi knew was that her stomach was upset all the time. This, on top of everything else, was a horrid blow for Anne.

Just when she most desperately needed it, Harry Harrison—who had first mentioned Ireland to her—recommended Anne to the UK publisher Futura as author for a trilogy of children's books dealing with dinosaurs. Anthony Cheetham, the publisher, agreed. The advance was very welcome and Harry's kindness was never forgotten.

In the midst of all this, Anne had to write the story for NESFA Press. Finally, in the throes of a terrible bout of bronchitis, she wondered how she would ever find *a time when* she could write it. With that thought came the title "A Time When," and with the title Anne found the story.

There was one major hitch to Anne's attendance at Boskone and the subsequent signing tour: Gigi. The signing tour would last far beyond Gigi's Easter vacation, and Anne could afford neither the additional airfare nor the lodging. Fortunately, Anne found an excellent solution, again at Brennanstown.

Many of Brennanstown's riders were students teaching and studying for their British Horse Society Assistant Instructorship, known as the AI. It was the principal credential required to work with horses. Anne discovered that one of the students, Antoinette O'Connell, was in need of lodgings. Antoinette, "Anto" for short, got on famously with the reduced family. She soon moved in, taking my room, and providing Gigi with a "big sister."

That problem solved, Anne put the finishing touches on her trip, corrected the galleys for "A Time When," packed her mother's ashes in my old fake-elephant-hide camera bag, and left for Boston. As she was packing to go, Gigi asked if she could carry anything. Anne handed her the camera bag.

"What's in it?" Gigi asked.

"Mother," Anne replied simply. Gigi let out an "eek" and nearly dropped it.

In Boston, the Customs officer opened the camera bag and asked, "What's this?"

"Mother," Anne said again. When he looked puzzled, she added, "Her remains."

He dropped that bag faster than Gigi had. "Lady, I don't know if you can do that!"

"Oh, yes, I can, and here's the documentation." And she passed over all the papers necessary for the importation of her mother's ashes. The supervisor had to be called, but at last the papers were found to be in order and Anne was allowed into the United States with her mother.

Because of all the Customs foofaraw, Anne was nearly the last person out. I was the first one to see her. She was hauling a lot of stuff, so I said, "Is there anything I can carry?" I was surprised when she handed me my old camera bag.

I looked at it curiously. "What's in this?"

"Mother," she said again. I clutched that bag tight in my arms. I'm sure that Bami would have loved the whole thing.

The next day, cool and foggy, we drove to the cemetery with Anne's aunt Edna, her cousin Joe Gibney, and Alec. In a short ceremony, Bami was laid to rest next to her husband, G. H. McCaffrey. On the way back, Edna said, "Now GH takes on the white man's burden once more."

Boskone was a wonderful tonic for Anne. "A Time When" sold well and she won the E. E. "Doc" Smith Award. The signing tour was a success.

Better yet, the Ballantines' years of patiently keeping their authors' books on the shelves had begun to pay off handsomely for Anne. The March royalty check was regal: $4,500. Anne was overjoyed—she could afford to have the telephone turned back on.

But the best was yet to come. Beth Blish had started helping her mother, Virginia, in the agenting business. She met with Jean Karl, the editor at Atheneum, and heard a brilliant request: Was there any chance of Anne writing a story for young women in a different part of Pern? Jean felt that more female readers would be wooed to science fiction if they could identify with the characters.

When the question came to Anne back in Ireland, she pulled out the piece she had started to write for Roger Elwood, about a young woman named Menolly. At the time, back in Meadowbrook House, the words would not come; Anne had no one like Menolly from which to draw. Now, with the young Brennanstown riders constantly in sight, and often at dinner, Anne found inspiration: in the ebullient Derval Diamond, Kim Baker—who had taught her donkey to jump— and all the other students and riders.

Now the story of Menolly wanted to be written. Anne found that *Dragonsong* came to her quickly. With a house full of youngsters every evening, she had no lack of inspiring characters. For the character of Menolly, whom Anne had never been able to *see*, she found one in particular: Derval Diamond.

Anne signed the contract in 1975 and *Dragonsong* was published in 1976. Even before it was published, Jean Karl wrote to ask Anne for a sequel—at the same time that Anne wrote Jean Karl asking if she could! They quickly agreed; the book would be *Dragonsinger*.

Once again, as things were looking up in her writing, things were falling down at home. The house we had been renting started showing worrisome cracks along the main wall that ran the length of the house. Anne informed the owners, who called in an architect. The architect was amazed to discover that the center wall rested on *nothing*! There were no supports, no underflooring, nothing. The weight of the center wall was beginning to pull the house down. Worse, the house had been built upon fill, which was subsiding, so that the house was beginning to slip downhill while also breaking in the middle.

Even if she had wanted to, Anne could not stay in 79 Shanganagh Vale. She had been happy in the house and hated the thought of starting another round of annual moves. She counted up her earnings and was surprised to find that she could afford a down payment on a house.

To get a house, Anne needed a loan. She approached her bank manager with a copy of the letter from Atheneum, stating the advance monies she was to be paid for the paperback sale. She remembers watching the bank manager reading the letter when she heard, "A woman shouldn't be allowed to have this much money."

The bank manager's lips hadn't moved. Anne realized that the exchange had to have been telepathic. She thanked him for his time, took back her letter, and changed banks. She got her mortgage from the Irish Permanent Building Society.

She found her house twenty-six miles outside of Dublin, in the southern county of Wicklow, just about nine miles south of the new Brennanstown Riding School. The house had been built by the next-door neighbors. The Beirnes had built the house for their mother, who lived in Northern Ireland, but she had decided that even with all that was going on in Belfast, she just couldn't leave her friends. The house was separated from theirs by a tall wall. It was a four-bedroom bungalow with an L-shaped living/dining room and a cozy kitchen. It stood on a full third of an acre. It was love at first sight.

Anne named it Dragonhold, because her dragons had bought it for her.

Dragonhold from the air

The Dragon's Head

*Jan Regan (Lessa) exercising a pony
in front of Dragonhold*

*Gigi with our dog Saffron at
Dragonhold*

We loved that house so much that we moved in the night before the carpeting was put in and slept in front of the fireplace— Gigi, myself, Anto, Rick Farmer, and Eamonn Hanrahan, all huddled in blankets.

Dragonhold came together quickly as a warm, friendly household. Anne's master carpenter friend, Wayne Sheader, made a present of some driftwood he had found on the seashore that he'd embellished just slightly to become a dragon's head, which we placed in the bushes outside to frighten the unwary.

Anne had realized that she could build stables on the side of Dragonhold. Soon Ed was installed, along with Gigi's horse, Ben. Ed got to play in a field not far from the house and got happily fat eating grass and frolicking whenever he felt like it. He'd always come when Anne called "Horseface!"

Settled in, Anne picked up where "A Time When" left off and finished *The White Dragon*. Judy-Lynn del Rey and everyone at Ballantine/Del Rey loved it. They were glad to get their first new dragon book in seven years. They got Michael Whelan, whose magnificent art was always eye-catching, to do a matching set of covers and rereleased *Dragonflight* and *Dragonquest* in their new covers at the same time as they published *The White Dragon* in hardback.

When it came out in 1978, *The White Dragon* flew high enough to become the first science fiction hardcover book to reach the *New York Times* bestseller list.

The success of *The White Dragon* gave Anne, who had made the dragons fly, a secure perch on the ground.

*A*nne had always been amazed to find people who *belonged* in her books, like Jan Regan and Bernard Shattuck. And she had often used characteristics of the people she knew in her people on Pern. In all those years, Anne had never directly *put* someone in her books. "They've got their own lives; I don't need to give them more," she said. But when tragedy struck, she changed her rule.

With her greater economic freedom, Anne found herself able to afford the "little" things in life—a new car, good saddles, and other tack for her horse. She bought a Toyota Corolla and has been a firm Toyota fan ever since.

The new tack and the Corolla brought Anne some unwanted attention. One night the family was startled by noises out back, but as the wind often brought strange sounds, no one thought much of it. It was not until the next morning that they discovered that the tack room had been burgled. Immediately afterward, Anne applied for and got a license for a shotgun. The daughter of the Kernel, Anne knew full well how to load and fire a shotgun.

Gigi was now the only one at home—I was doing a stint in the US Army—and old enough to throw the occasional party. Gigi and I had been having parties since 1971, and had always been good about behaving and cleaning up afterward. However, this one night the party was crashed by some rowdies who would not listen to common sense. Fortunately, another of the party-goers had a bit of a reputation himself and was outraged that anyone would abuse Anne's hospitality. John Greene threw the rowdies out.

John was then just finishing off an enlistment in the Irish Army. When I met him while on leave, we compared experiences: we ran two miles in tennis shoes, they ran five miles every day in full pack; we had the finest equipment in the world, they had whatever the French or British didn't want anymore; we had to be prepared to fight off the Soviets, they were prepared to fight off all comers. I decided that the Irish Army was a tougher outfit.

Johnny's sense of humor and readiness to "try it on" meant that he had had many a rough-and-ready tumble. He was not someone to be trifled with.

He and Anne clicked. They understood and truly admired each other. Johnny once told me, "Your Mum is so fantastic. She really cares. I would do anything for her. I'd guard her door. I would die for her."

I did not escape Johnny's sense of humor. When I got out of the Army, my mother realized that I did not have a decent suit to wear. As she had just gotten membership in the very posh Sloane Club in London, she was determined that her son would be presentable; my mother gets a real kick out of "presenting" her boys (it's the only time she can get me in a suit).

Johnny had just left the Irish Army himself and was, surprisingly, working in a haberdashery. So I was sent to him. He picked out a

Dragonhold, seen from the exercise area

stylish gray pinstripe. When I complained to him that it was too loose, he looked me up and down and said, "When's the last time you exercised?" I mumbled something and Johnny said with a knowing look, "Trust me, Todd, it'll fit you."

All too soon, it did. And now I'm far too large for it.

d got older and feebler. Finally, after he had a series of mini-strokes, Anne decided that Ed's pains were greater than his pleasures. The vet came and administered the drug and Anne, with tears streaming, said good-bye to Mr. Ed.

The rest of the day was hard for her. At 11:20 P.M., Irish time, Anne was awakened by the phone. It was Alec, announcing the birth of Eliza Oriana Johnson, Anne's first grandchild. The date was memorable: 9 September 1981—the last square date of the century, 9/9/81.

*I*t was about that same year that Johnny started getting into more trouble. "I just can't make it in the real world," he told me not long after I finished my term in the Army.

"Well, what are you going to do, reenlist in the Irish Army?" I asked.

"Do you think the Americans would take me?" he countered. I didn't realize that he was half-serious.

Not long after, Johnny told us how he had stopped his little brother from entering the French Foreign Legion. And then I got this letter,

> *Hello Todd,*
>
> *I suppose you'll laugh yourself silly to learn that I've joined the French Foreign Legion.*

He was right.

For the next several years Johnny would regale us with letters from such far-off places as Djibouti. "It's 40°C here in the desert and they're dropping like flies. You get used to attending a funeral every week, but I think it's too much when the medical officer drops dead halfway through a 40-kilometer march."

And he was a good soldier. Soon Johnny was sporting corporal's chevrons. And then he was promoted again, to the lofty "Marèchal de Logique," which is equivalent to sergeant. He worked as a radio tech and had to become fluent in French, although we never heard him speak the language.

He knew that Anne did her shopping in Bray on Thursdays and would often surprise her there when home on leave.

In November 1988, John Greene was murdered, for no apparent reason, while out for the evening in Orange, France. Anne felt his loss keenly—we all did—and decided that she would make him Jayge (for "J.G.," one of his nicknames) in *Renegades of Pern*. She dedicated the book to him. Since then, Anne has put him in every book she writes, in hopes of giving him alternate lives for the one he lost.

John Greene,
Marèchal de Logique

She asked me especially to remember him in this book. I've done my best, but really to understand John Greene and how much he meant to Anne, you'd have to read one of her earliest stories, written even before John was born. Somehow, inexplicably, she captured the essence of her future admiration for John Greene in "The Ship Who Sang."

N ow you have the stories behind the stories. Just as Anne has more tales still to be told, you can be sure that there are still more stories behind the stories. We'll all have to wait and see.

Thank you for taking the time to learn the stories behind the stories, and I hope you enjoyed seeing how Anne McCaffrey, the "dragonlady," first set the dragons free on Pern and then was herself freed by her dragons—and by you, their fans.

May your skies always be bright and full of promise.